About Last Night...
by Morgan Cutter

Okay, so I know I made one of the biggest mistakes a woman can make last night when I let my brother's best friend kiss me senseless. Especially since Wyatt McCall has been the bane of my existence for the past twenty years! It must have been those two (three?) glasses of champagne I had...on top of that cold medicine. Of course, it also could have been a reaction to seeing my brother get married, but mind you, I'm not about to admit that to anyone else. And even though there are still three more weddings to go, this is *never* going to happen again. Even if *that kiss* superseded my wildest dreams...

Dear Reader,

Who doesn't love a wedding? And if you're single, you just naturally start thinking about your own love life and who you might someday end up with. So is it any wonder that when Morgan Cutler, the heroine of Marie Ferrarella's *A Match for Morgan*, starts making the rounds of all her siblings' weddings, she finds herself thinking a few thoughts of love? What amazes her, though, is the identity of the man she's thinking about. She and Wyatt McCall have been at odds ever since she can remember, so why is he suddenly looking awfully…kissable? You'll hate to say goodbye to THE CUTLERS OF THE SHADY LADY RANCH, but I think you'll agree with me that this miniseries is going out with a real bang.

Then check out Lynn Miller's *Did You Say* Baby?! Take one cowboy who knows *nothing* about babies, add one heroine with a baby in tow and no working knowledge of cowboys, stick them together in one suddenly-too-small house out on the ranch and…boom! Spontaneous combustion is bound to occur. This is only Lynn's second book, but she knows her stuff, and you'll be looking forward to more from her, I promise.

So have fun, and don't forget to come back next month for two more wonderful Yours Truly novels, the books all about unexpectedly meeting—and marrying—Mr. Right.

Yours,

Leslie Wainger
Executive Senior Editor

Please address questions and book requests to:
Silhouette Reader Service
U.S.: 3010 Walden Ave., P.O. Box 1325, Buffalo, NY 14269
Canadian: P.O. Box 609, Fort Erie, Ont. L2A 5X3

MARIE FERRARELLA

A Match for Morgan

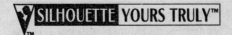

Published by Silhouette Books
America's Publisher of Contemporary Romance

To June Casey—
the best part of your life
is still ahead of you.
Trust me.

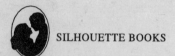

SILHOUETTE BOOKS

ISBN 0-373-52087-5

A MATCH FOR MORGAN

Copyright © 1999 by Marie Rydzynski-Ferrarella

Dear Reader,

Well, here we are, seemingly at the end of the Cutler saga. I say "seemingly" because you never know with these books. When you least expect it, one of the characters seeps into another book, making it his or her own. That's one of the things I love about writing, the surprises. They happen to the writer as well as the reader.

I left Morgan's story for last not just because she's the youngest, but because Morgan wasn't the kind to go running off, losing her heart, until all those around her were losing theirs. Stubborn, headstrong and feisty, she needed someone strong to help her find her place in that wonderland called love. She met her match in Wyatt McCall. And though she tried to deny them, the tender feelings she'd been harboring for Wyatt for so long were overwhelming in the face of one wedding after another.

I truly hope you had half as much fun reading about the Cutlers as I had writing about them. And now, off to the next saga. Meet me there?

Love,

Marie Ferrarella

Stop on by
The Shady Lady Ranch
in Serendipity, Montana,
home of the Cutler brood—five siblings finding love in the most unexpected places!

Zoe McKay m. Jake Cutler

├── Will Cutler m. Denise Cavanaugh

├── Quint Cutler m. Ginny Marlow

├── Kent Cutler m. Brianne Gainsborough

├── Hank Cutler m. Fiona Reilly

└── Morgan Cutler m. Wyatt McCall

WILL AND THE HEADSTRONG FEMALE
(Yours Truly, 11/98)

THE LAW AND GINNY MARLOW
(Yours Truly, 1/99)

COWBOYS ARE FOR LOVING
(Yours Truly, 9/98)

FIONA AND THE SEXY STRANGER
(Yours Truly, 7/98)

A MATCH FOR MORGAN
(Yours Truly, 3/99)

1

"**Y**ou can't be serious."

Staring at the name she saw neatly written on the list her brother Hank had just handed her, Morgan Cutler turned to look at him. This was a hell of a surprise to spring on her. She'd thought that Wyatt McCall was a safe distance away, not here, waiting to breathe down her neck.

Maybe there was some explanation. She mentally crossed her fingers as she repeated, "Tell me you're not serious."

Hank leaned back in his chair, balancing himself on the two rear legs. They were in the kitchen of their parents' sprawling ranch house. The large room, decorated in wood and stone, had practically been the center of their lives when they were growing up. There was always something comforting about the kitchen. All the major decisions affecting them had been made in this room. It seemed only fitting that he discuss the plans for his wedding here—the first of four weddings the Cutlers would see in what promised to be a very frantic September.

Hank laced his hands behind his blond head, his mouth twitching only slightly as he tried vainly to keep the grin off his face. Because the teasing and pranks of childhood weren't all that many years removed, he feigned ignorance.

"About Fiona, definitely." The grin grew larger. "About the wedding, yes."

Morgan's blue eyes narrowed, warning the youngest of her four older brothers that she was in no mood to be toyed with.

"Don't get cute with me, Henry Alan Cutler. I mean about having Wyatt in the wedding party. I thought he was still in Hawaii, impressing everyone there with his so-called business acumen."

"He's back. His firm transferred him to take over the Programming Division here. He's staying with his folks until he finds a place of his own. Even if he hadn't transferred, he told me that there's no way he would miss my wedding."

Morgan sighed. There was no mistake, no hope to cling to. Wyatt was back. "Lucky you."

Hank leaned forward, planting his chair on solid ground again. The war between Morgan and Wyatt was an old, on-going thing. "Morgan, Wyatt's my best friend."

Morgan shook her head. Damn it, why did he have to come back now? Why couldn't Wyatt have lost touch with her brothers the way so many friends do when they move away?

"I always said you should set your sights higher than ground level, Hank. All you'll ever find there are snakes, slithering around, waiting to bite you when you least expect it."

Hank took back his list of the wedding party and folded it before tucking it into his shirt pocket. "Shouldn't you have outgrown this by now?"

Morgan tossed her head, sending a sheet of long blond hair flying over her shoulder. "Feuds are ageless, you know that," she said, tongue in cheek. "Besides, your best friend is more to blame in this than I am. He can hardly say a civil word to me whenever he enters a room."

"That's because you won't let him," he reminded her. "You attack as soon as you see him coming."

It was safer that way. She wasn't about to let Wyatt McCall catch her at a disadvantage like he had that evening, five years ago. Not ever again. She'd made a point of not being around when Wyatt was. His move to Hawaii had made things a lot easier for her when she visited her parents' ranch. But there was no way she was about to share that with Hank. As far as her brothers and parents were concerned, this was just a continuation of a feud that had begun one snowy day two decades ago.

So, she merely shrugged carelessly. "Dad always said the best defense is a strong offense."

Getting up, Hank laughed. "And you can give offense better than anyone I know." Because he'd taken an early flight from Bedford, California, to return to his parents' Montana ranch and had missed lunch, he opened the refrigerator to see what he could eat to tide him over until dinner was ready. Everything that met his eye looked healthy. He was in the mood for rich and filling. Sighing, he settled on an apple.

Morgan stood on her toes and ruffled his hair, knowing he hated having it mussed. "Behave, or I won't give you your wedding present."

He raised one hand, palm up, in surrender. "I'll be good."

"That'll be the day." She supposed it wouldn't be so bad. After all, it wasn't as if she and Wyatt were going to be chained at the hip. There were a lot of people coming. Half the town, if her father had his way. She could easily avoid Wyatt. "Speaking of 'the day,' it's your day, your wedding, you should be able to have it the way you want it."

"Are you actually saying you don't mind having Wyatt in the wedding party?"

"Oh, I mind all right. But I'll just have to make the best of it." Trust the man to complicate her life at the worst moment, Morgan thought.

Obviously surprised, Hank recovered quickly and brushed a brotherly kiss against her cheek before taking a bite of his apple. "Knew I could count on you, Morg."

"Of course you can. It's Wyatt McCall you have to worry about in this mix, not me." Taking the apple from him, Morgan took a healthy bite out of it before handing it back. "I'll behave myself."

"That's all I ask, Morgan."

She thought of Wyatt and wondered who he was bringing to the wedding, then shrugged away the thought. Made no difference to her if he brought every last cheerleader from the Dallas Cowboys lineup. No difference at all.

Taking the list out of Hank's breast pocket, she looked at it again. "Well, at least you had enough sense not to make him your best man."

"That spot belongs to Will."

Hank was close to all of them, but everyone knew and understood that there was a bond between him and his oldest brother that was just a shade stronger than the rest. Morgan nodded.

"Let's see, Will's your best man and Quint, Kent and Peter—" she enumerated her other brothers and Fiona's brother-in-law "—are your ushers. I guess Wyatt fits into the slot of what, subhuman agitator?"

Hank took the list from her, this time sliding it into his back pocket. "Don't start, Morg."

"Start?" She looked at him innocently, then grinned. If she couldn't avoid this, then she'd damn well have fun with it. "I never start anything."

"Yeah, right. And birds take taxis to go south for the winter." His grin turned serious around the edges. "A word to the wise, Morgan. If you ruin Fiona's day, I'll hunt you down and shoot you."

Morgan laughed, patting his shoulder. They both knew she'd rather die than ruin something so important to him. "You couldn't track an elephant across a muddy clearing, but as long as you don't pair me off with Wyatt, you've got nothing to worry about."

Hank closed his eyes and sighed.

Morgan had an uneasy feeling erupt in the pit of her stomach. But before she could put her suspicions in the form of a question, their mother walked in.

Zoe Cutler looked like an older, slightly shorter version of her daughter. Slight, but not delicate. Zoe had the same aura of determination that Morgan possessed. The only difference at a quick first glance was her hair. Once long like Morgan's, Zoe now wore it in a fashionable short blond cut that needed a minimum of fussing.

She gave her only daughter a scrutinizing look just as her husband entered the kitchen behind her. She'd caught enough of the exchange between Morgan and Hank to know what this was about. And she knew Morgan well enough to guess that there was something else at the root of all this, something that was years in the making. Eventually, it would come to a head. But one way or another, Zoe wasn't about to let it upset the first wedding they'd had on the Cutler ranch in thirty-five years.

"Morgan, don't give your brother grief." Going to the cupboard, she took out two large pots from under the counter and placed each on the stove. "It's hard enough for a man to plan a wedding, any wedding, much less one that's being held a long distance from where he's living without you adding to his problems."

"I wouldn't dream of it." Morgan flashed a smile in greeting at her father. "However, I can't speak for Wyatt."

Kissing first her mother's cheek, then her father's, Morgan settled down at the table again, the picture of serenity. It was only underneath that things were churning. She'd thought, hoped really, that Wyatt would stay put in Hawaii and let her enjoy this special occasion without being disturbed. And having him around definitely disturbed her.

An army of spices and ingredients began forming on the counter adjacent to the stove as Zoe prepared to create another evening meal.

"Speaking of Wyatt," Zoe began nonchalantly, "he called yesterday and said something about taking us all out to dinner the night before the wedding." Hands temporarily stilled, she glanced over her shoulder, her words directed toward Hank, her eyes on Morgan to see her daughter's reaction. "That was rather nice of Wyatt, don't you think?"

"Nice," Morgan echoed, then groaned inwardly. Dinner. Terrific. The man was going to be perpetually in her face for the duration.

"I always did like that boy," Jake interjected.

Easy for him to say, Morgan thought. He'd never made a fool of himself in front of Wyatt. "You always were too easy, Dad," Morgan quipped.

Humor lit his eyes. "Let *you* slide with a lot of stuff, missy, didn't I?"

Her eyes crinkled as she laughed, tossing her blond mane over her shoulder again. She came up behind her father and wrapped her arms around one of his, laying her head against it the way she used to when she was small and tried to wield a favor out of him after her mother had turned her down.

She batted her lashes at him when he looked down at her face. "That was because I was your baby girl and had you wrapped around my little finger."

"You got that right." Jake gave his daughter a fond squeeze. It was incredible how much she reminded him of Zoe when he'd first met her. "But you weren't supposed to know that."

Morgan raised her chin, her mouth spreading in what was recognized as a Cutler grin. She dearly loved this man. Loved all of them with a fierceness that was almost unimaginable.

"I was your *smart* baby girl." Morgan nodded toward her brother. "It was Hank here who was the dumb one."

Zoe stopped mixing. She normally didn't press her children, but her curiosity was at its limit. This so-called feud went far beyond childish tomfoolery. "What *is* it you have against Wyatt?"

For years Zoe had thought Wyatt McCall might be the very thing that her headstrong, obstinate daughter needed. Morgan had a heart of gold, like her father, but a stubborn will of iron that outdid any of her brothers, even Kent. She needed a strong hand in hers, someone she could respect, not boss around. There were times Zoe despaired that her youngest child would never find a man who could make her release her grasp on the reins of control long enough to share them. Zoe knew how important that was to a marriage, to share and not just control or be controlled.

The only man Zoe had ever met outside the family who seemed equal to the job was Wyatt. If only Morgan would stop snapping every time they came close to each other.

Morgan pretended to think. Her reason was too personal to share, even with the people who mattered most to her. "Alphabetically, or shall I just spew it at random?"

Zoe merely shook her head. "Any way you want."

Morgan ticked faults off on her fingers. "He's egotistical, obnoxious, annoying—"

"Sally Gibson doesn't seem to think so," Zoe cut in, then noted with interest that there was a rather green light coming into her daughter's eyes. It gave her hope. "Saw her hanging on his arm the other day. Hanging all over him, actually. She looked awfully happy to see he was back."

Morgan waved the information away with a condescending snort. "Sally Gibson has the IQ of a jar of pickles. Even if he does take notice of her, she'll be history soon enough. It's a given that Wyatt never hangs around long. He was only married to Judith, what, six minutes?"

"Over two and a half years, almost three," Zoe corrected, though she knew it wasn't necessary. Morgan knew exactly how long Wyatt's marriage had lasted. And that the breakup was one of the reasons Wyatt had taken the Hawaii assignment.

"He's just being young and enjoying himself now," Jake pointed out. Zoe raised an eyebrow in his direction. "Not that I'd know anything about that," Jake added quickly, pressing his lips together to keep from chuckling.

Morgan saw the look that passed between her parents. Together forever and they still behaved like they were dating, just on the cusp of that first wild love. God, but she'd give anything to have someone love her that way—and to love someone the way her mother loved her father.

Still, she couldn't resist teasing. "So you didn't enjoy yourself when you were a young man?"

"I was with your mother from the time I was eighteen—" Jake began to explain before he realized what that had to sound like. "You know what I mean." He tugged on the ends of Morgan's hair the way he'd once tugged on her ponytail. "Why are you trying to get me into trouble, girl?"

She wrapped her arms around him. "Because it's the only fun I have these days."

"Now that's hard to believe." The back door slammed shut, underlining the words Wyatt had just uttered. He walked into the kitchen, making himself at home the way he'd done for over twenty years. His own parents' house had been larger, more elegant, but the neighboring Cutlers' place was warmer. Nicer.

He'd always liked coming here more than he'd liked returning to his own home. He knew his brother Casey felt the same way. There was a warmth here. His family was civil, polite, but the Cutlers really cared about one another. It was evident in everything they did, even when words flew hot and fast between them.

He took off his hat and casually hung it on the back of the closest chair. It pleased him that he'd taken Morgan by surprise. Nodding at Hank, he greeted the older Cutlers before looking down at Morgan.

When he did, his smile was ever-so-slightly superior, knowing that it incensed her. "Hello, Morgan, didn't know you'd be here."

She prided herself on being able to hit the ground running, and recovered quickly enough. Her smile was tight as she looked at the man who'd been the burr under her saddle from the first moment she'd laid eyes on him.

No, the second moment, she amended mentally, being honest with herself. The first moment she'd seen him, standing so tall with a snowdrift behind him, she'd actually experienced what could only be termed an insane, girlish infatuation. But she'd been just shy of five at the time and couldn't be faulted for having a lapse in judgment. The flying snowballs that followed, crashing into her face as Wyatt laughed at catching her offguard had quickly squelched those tender, misguided feelings. Tender feelings that were destined to become even more misguided a decade and a half later.

She'd tried to get even that winter, but couldn't. Not then. He'd had a better arm than hers, but she'd practiced all year, using rocks for snowballs and tin cans as her target. She'd gotten him good the following winter.

And he'd gotten her good that summer, five years ago, a small voice seemed to whisper in her head. The thought irritated Morgan, like nettles being drawn across a tender palm.

"Hello, Wyatt, I could say the same to you." Her smile never faltered. "What's the matter, Hawaii decide to clear out the undesirables from their shores?"

"Morgan," Zoe chided sharply.

"Sorry, just being curious," Morgan murmured.

Wyatt smiled indulgently at Morgan, making her feel suddenly very feline. "That's all right, Mrs. Cutler. Let her have her fun. Like she said, she has very little of it." He leaned over and in a stage whisper added, "Maybe if you polished up your manners, that wouldn't be true."

Morgan struggled not to shiver as his breath zipped along her flesh. Something hot and demanding tightened within her. She glared as she watched Wyatt open the refrigerator and help himself to a soda, as if he belonged here. He didn't. He belonged somewhere far away. Somewhere where the sight of him couldn't remind her what an idiot she'd once been.

She looked at him, wishing he'd gotten ugly. Or at least plain. Why did the man have to get better looking with time? Why couldn't he be developing a spare tire, or going to seed? Why did he have to look so much like...like Wyatt?

Restless, she took a napkin out of the holder in the center of the table and toyed with it. "I hear

Hank's decided to pay me back for past transgressions by putting us both in the wedding party.''

Wyatt turned from the refrigerator, his dark eyes sweeping over her. It had been a little more than two years since he'd last seen her. Was it his imagination, or was she sexier looking than he remembered? Didn't seem fair in his opinion, to package something that was so fiery to look like sweet candy.

His eyes shifted to Hank before looking at Morgan again. "I hear the same thing. Personally, I'm looking at it as penance." He took a long drag of the soda, looking at her over the can. "You do something different with your hair?"

Morgan raised her chin, waiting for the punch line. "No."

He shrugged. "Pity."

Morgan knew he was just trying to provoke her. "A word that you are on the receiving end of a great deal, I'd imagine. Speaking of the wedding, I hope you don't intend to embarrass Hank." She rose, crossing to the refrigerator herself. She elbowed Wyatt out of the way. Was that a new cologne he was wearing? Morgan took out a can of soda for herself. "Try to remember not to drag your knuckles on the floor when you walk down the aisle with whatever poor unfortunate bridesmaid winds up being paired off with you." The can fizzed as she popped the top.

Wyatt raised an inquisitive brow as he caught Hank's eye.

He had to tell her, Hank thought. It was only right. Besides, if he waited until it became evident to her at the wedding rehearsal, she'd probably kill him, witnesses or no witnesses.

Hank took a deep breath. "Morg."

Sitting down again, Morgan stiffened. She knew that tone. It was the one Hank used when he was about to tell her something he knew she wasn't going to like hearing. *Oh please don't let it be what I think it is.*

Morgan gave Hank the most intimidating look she could summon. "Hank, you'd better just be clearing your throat."

Zoe came to her son's rescue. This was going to take more finesse than Hank had at his disposal.

"Morgan, Fiona was kind enough to include your brothers' fiancées in the wedding party." Morgan looked at her mother. She already knew that. And then came the information she didn't want. "There'll be Quint with Ginny, Kent with Brianne—she's flying in from New York—and because Fiona's sister is matron of honor, Denise is going to be paired off with Bridgette's husband, Peter."

That just left her and…

Morgan looked from her mother to Hank and saw the guilty look. Oh, God, this really was going to be penance, wasn't it?

She took hold of Hank's arm, pinning him in place in case he thought of bolting. "Why can't I be paired off with Bridgette's husband?"

The reason was a very basic one. "Because in high heels you'll be taller than he is, and he's sensitive about his height."

What about her sensitivity? she wanted to demand. But she knew that Wyatt would be convulsed at the mere mention that she was sensitive. She wasn't about to add to his entertainment.

"I'll walk barefoot," she offered, knowing it was futile.

"You'll walk with Wyatt," Jake said firmly, then his tone softened. "It's just for an evening," he reminded her.

There was no way out of this. If she said no, she'd be the one causing the schism in the family, not Wyatt, damn him. She had to agree.

"The longest damn evening of my life," she told Hank grudgingly.

Wyatt couldn't resist. Hands on the back of her chair, he leaned over and whispered, "Only if you're lucky," close to her ear.

As smooth as a cat, she stood up. Still leaning on the chair, Wyatt nearly fell backward when she took her anchoring weight from it. He regained his balance at the last moment.

Hank shut his eyes and moaned. "I'm beginning to think I should have eloped."

"Don't even joke about it," Zoe warned.

Morgan whirled around to face Hank. She grabbed his arm, pretending to pull him toward the front door. "I'll drive you to the airport."

"Morgan." Zoe's soft features were drawn into a warning frown.

Morgan dropped Hank's arm. "It's his day, he should have it the way he wants," she said innocently.

"Exactly." The no-nonsense look on Zoe's face intensified.

Morgan sighed. Having to pair off with Wyatt was going to really put a definite damper on the festivities, but she was going to have to be equal to it.

"Not to worry, Mrs. Cutler," Wyatt volunteered easily, eyeing Morgan. "I'll keep her in line."

Wyatt knew that he was giving himself a lot of credit. He'd probably have an easier time keeping a wildcat in line, but he liked the fire that came into her eyes whenever she was angry. Too bad they kept finding themselves on opposite sides so often. Otherwise...

But there was no otherwise, and maybe it was better that way. For all of them.

Morgan turned on him, hands on hips. Keep her in line? The gall, the unmitigated gall. "You and what army?"

God help him but there was something appealing about Morgan whenever she got angry like this, Wyatt thought. He figured there had to be a little insanity in everyone for him to feel that way about someone who'd just as soon see him drawn and quartered than draw another breath.

"That'll be decided when the time comes," he told her.

Zoe changed the subject. "Stay for dinner, Wyatt?"

Wyatt's smile was genial. Morgan's mother cooked better than anyone he knew, even the woman his parents had hired. "Don't mind if I do, Mrs. Cutler."

When Morgan crossed to the doorway, motorcycle helmet in hand, Zoe looked at her daughter accusingly. "Where are you going?"

"Home." In her present frame of mind, Morgan knew it was better for everyone all around if she left now before she said something she would really regret. Not that she would regret it, Morgan amended, but Hank and her parents might. She never said anything to Wyatt that was unjustified and unmerited. "It's a long ride back."

"I thought you said you were staying for dinner," Jake said. The look on her father's face asked her to stay.

She really didn't want to leave, didn't want to be driven out of the place she would always think of as home no matter where she went, but she knew if she stayed, she would risk losing her temper.

Morgan shook her head. "Change of plans."

She looked directly at Wyatt. "Besides, I do have a lot of paperwork to catch up on if I'm going to take part of Friday off."

Wyatt surprised her by blocking her exit, one hand on each side of the doorjamb. Morgan raised her chin. "I'll walk right over you if you don't get out of my way," she warned.

She would, too, he thought. "I don't want to drive you away from your mother's table, Morgan. I can eat here some other time."

Morgan's eyes narrowed. Oh, no, he wasn't going to be the good guy here. They liked him too much already.

"Don't flatter yourself, Wyatt. If I wanted to eat here, I would. You don't affect anything I do, one way or the other." It was a lie, but a necessary one. "But it's a long ride back to Butte, and I should get started." Turning, she backtracked to kiss her father's cheek. "I'd see about putting a new lock on the doors if I were you, Dad. You really don't want to leave yourself open to having Hawaii's undesirables drift in and out."

"At least let me get you something to take home." Zoe began to pull open the refrigerator door.

But Morgan stopped her. "I am taking something home, Ma. It's called indigestion."

And then Morgan saw the look on Hank's face. Despite his teasing words, he was worried. Her mother was right, he had enough on his mind without her adding to it. It was bad enough that she was upset by this turn of events. There was no point in adding to Hank's anxiety. He wanted Wyatt in his wedding, and he should have things the way he wanted. Even if it killed her.

Morgan patted Hank's cheek affectionately on her way out.

"Don't worry, big brother. I won't be the one who spoils your day." She glanced over her shoulder, her last remark aimed at Wyatt, who'd retreated out of her way. "You might think about throwing yourself on your sword before next Sunday. It'd be the first honorable thing you've ever done." Her complacent smile encompassed the other three people in the room. "'Bye, family."

Wyatt merely grinned as he heard the front door open and then close again. "Nice to know you can still depend on some things staying the same," he murmured under his breath.

Zoe heard him and smiled to herself. Maybe it would be just a matter of time. After all, there were three more weddings after Hank's.

2

"I guess this isn't supposed to be an actual dress rehearsal, is it? Or is that what you're planning to wear to the wedding?" Wyatt's green eyes swept over Morgan as she hurried up the church steps.

Just her luck, Morgan thought. He *would* be standing on the church steps just as she roared into the parking lot on her motorcycle. By the look of the cars that were already in the lot, everyone else had gotten here ahead of her.

It figured.

Morgan'd barely had time to remove her helmet and hadn't waited to catch her breath as she took the steps two at a time to the front of the church. As was happening more and more frequently in her life, the morning hadn't been long enough. She'd been far from finished with her caseload when she'd finally all but shot out of the third-floor office.

Though she was in a hurry, there was still a case lingering on her mind all the way from Butte to Serendipity. Try as she might, she couldn't get a small boy's tear-streaked, trusting face out of her mind. Josh Miller, all of four and suddenly all alone in the world. She and Josh had built a relationship since she'd been the social worker assigned to his case. Working diligently over the past six months, she'd finally placed him with a foster family, Ann and Ray Johnson, two very nice people she could personally vouch for.

But even as she left him in their care early this morning, he'd clung to her. He'd been so afraid to start all over again.

"Stay with me, Morgan," he'd pleaded. She had literally felt her heart being pulled toward him.

The very last thing she was in the mood for right now was some of Wyatt's so-called levity. But that didn't seem to stop him as he kept staring at her. "Not that you don't look good in leather in a girl-rebel sort of way...."

Morgan glared at him as she moved past him to yank open one of the doors leading into the church.

She tossed her head, trying to get some of the body back into her hair without being too obvious. A motorcycle suited her needs far better than a car, but as with everything, there was a price to pay. In this case, it was flattened hair.

And then she stopped in mid-motion, helmet tucked under one arm, and turned around to look at him. Had he just said what she thought he did?

"Did something happen to my hearing on the

way over here, or did you just give me a half-chewed-up compliment?''

He followed her inside, letting the door close behind him. ''Take them any way you can get 'em, Cutler. A lady with your sweet disposition isn't in line to get too many compliments.''

Late or not, she paused long enough to look up at him and bat her lashes. ''I have a very sweet disposition—when I'm around human beings.''

''Okay, that's enough. End of round two,'' Will announced coming out of the inner church. ''Match called off on account of rain.''

Laughing, Morgan turned toward her oldest brother. The eternally unflappable Will looked just a wee bit frayed around the edges. Was that because he was vicariously experiencing what his own prewedding tension would be like all too soon? Probably, she mused.

''They don't call off boxing matches if it rains, Will.''

Morgan's correction left Will unfazed. He'd long since learned to turn a deaf ear to over half the things his sister said. If she took it into her head, Morgan would have argued with a stone.

''They do when I'm refereeing.'' Will's expression sobered, looking from Wyatt to Morgan. ''Hank is nervous enough without having to hear you two go at it in the wings.''

Wyatt thought of his own far-from-perfect union. Any way he looked at it, his marriage had been just two inches short of a total fiasco, even in the very beginning. Hard thing to admit for a man who'd once secretly had great hopes.

He shrugged philosophically. "Might give him a preview of what married life is like."

Morgan took umbrage for Fiona at Wyatt's comment. There was no comparison between Judith and her almost-sister-in-law.

"What *your* married life was like," she said tersely. "Fiona isn't anything like your ex-pom-pom girl. She's perfect for him."

If asked now, Wyatt wouldn't have been able to explain exactly what had attracted him to Judith in the first place. Granted, she'd been sexy as hell, but he'd always thought of himself as intelligent enough to see past physical attributes. Something had blinded him that summer five years ago, rendering him temporarily insane. Then, when the consequences had materialized, he'd shouldered his responsibility and tried to make the best of it. The best had not been nearly good enough.

Though he would never have admitted it to her, Morgan had been right on the money when she'd told him he was marrying a life-size fashion doll. One who'd wanted and expected him to buy her all the accessories. Judith could go through money like a man went through a morning shower—quickly and without a second thought. She'd almost bankrupted him before he'd called a halt to their marriage.

The toll her spending had made on his finances was like adding insult to injury.

"Is Hank bad?" Morgan asked Will, looking concerned.

"Not to the casual observer," Will responded. But Will wasn't a casual observer. He knew his brothers and sister inside out. "But if you look closely, I think his grin is frozen in place."

Morgan bit her lower lip. "Maybe he's just very happy."

Wyatt had another take on that. "Maybe he's just catatonic."

What kind of a best friend was he, anyway? Morgan wondered. Wasn't he supposed to be there, encouraging Hank instead of loitering on the front steps of the church, waiting until she arrived so he could heckle her?

His guess had earned him a punch to the shoulder he wouldn't have felt had he not been looking straight at Morgan when she delivered it. Laughing, Wyatt was quick to cover her fisted hand with his own, stopping Morgan in case she wanted to deliver a second blow. They didn't have time for this.

"I'll go a few rounds with you after rehearsal, Rocky," Wyatt promised. Hands against her back, he gave her a small push toward the door. "Right now, you're late."

Morgan didn't like having him point out any of

her failings, however inconsequential. Anything that came from him she took as a criticism.

After twenty-five years around Morgan, Will could read his sister like a book. Moving quickly, he stepped between them. "Everybody's already inside, Morgan." Will nodded toward the inner nave. "They're just waiting for you to show up."

He didn't have to add "as always"; she heard it in Will's voice.

"Traffic," she muttered, striding into the church behind him and ahead of Wyatt. There was no point in elaborating about her day and Josh. She wasn't about to explain things around Wyatt.

Wyatt looked at the helmet she carried under her arm. She'd been tearing around on that motorcycle of hers ever since she'd turned eighteen. The woman brought new meaning to the phrase hell-on-wheels. He could still remember the first time he saw her on it. She'd been proud enough to burst. She'd bought it with her own money, money she'd been saving for years. Purchased secondhand, the motorcycle was her pride and joy. She babied it and treated it more like a pet than a mode of transportation. He could almost envy it.

"Someday," Wyatt said, addressing the back of her head, "you're going to fall off that damn thing and break your fool neck."

She took her place at the rear of the gathering. Her other brothers were all there, paired off with their fiancées. An empty feeling flittered through her, and she blocked it. Instead she concentrated on being annoyed at Wyatt. Gritting her teeth together, she half growled, half whispered in his ear.

"That's something that doesn't need to concern you. McCall."

Wyatt stood beside her, his arm brushing against hers as she shrugged out of her jacket. He watched her deposit her jacket and helmet into a pew, a blending of modern with timelessness. Though he wouldn't say it, he would have hated to see something happen to her.

Leaning toward her, Wyatt replied, "No, but you are my best friend's sister, and I wouldn't want to see him unhappy."

Morgan looked to see if he was serious. She wouldn't have ascribed one decent feeling to the man. "I'm touched."

"Yes," he said slowly, ignoring her sarcastic tone, "I've always said that."

Morgan swallowed a retort. Prickly, it stuck in her throat. She could either voice it and cause a scene right in the middle of Hank's wedding rehearsal, or keep her peace and let it ride. She chose the latter because she loved Hank and because she had no choice really. By her watch, they had already held up the rehearsal fifteen minutes for her.

But there was nothing stopping her from saying it later. And she promised herself that she would, given the first opportunity.

"Nice of you to join us, Morgan," Quint commented when Morgan and Wyatt took their places at the end of the line. Before his sister could say anything, he turned toward the man in the dark vest at the altar. ''I think we're ready to begin now, Padre.''

''Doing your Clint Eastwood imitation?'' Ginny Marlow asked the man she was going to marry in three week's time.

Quint grinned as his brother poked him in the ribs. ''Every chance I get.''

''She's sure got your number,'' Hank noted.

Love filled his voice as it often did these days. ''That she has.''

The exchange of looks between Quint and Ginny made Morgan's heart swell and ache at the same time. She was glad for Quint—really, truly glad for all of her brothers to have found the women who seemed so perfect for them all during this one phenomenal summer. They were hardly getting engaged before they were getting married. But she was sad at the same time, because something precious was changing, not once but four times. Despite the blasé facade she deliberately tendered to the world, Morgan didn't really do well with change. And now everything would.

She was sad, too, because in her heart, Morgan knew it would never happen to her. There would never be a special someone who would make her want to see that one face lying beside her, morning after morning. There would never be that special

someone who would make her want to hold just
one hand, evening after evening. She had never
lost her heart that way to anyone, not even once.
Her heart never stayed put long enough. She would
become attracted and then disinterested faster than
bread rose in the oven.

She supposed that her track record for relation-
ships rivaled Wyatt's.

Now there was a scary thought, Morgan realized, suppressing a shiver. The only difference between her and Wyatt was that there was no marriage in her past.

Or in her future.

"You look pensive." Wyatt's whisper, tickling
her ear, broke through her thoughts like a sudden
cloudburst over the desert.

Morgan could feel every single muscle in her
body tighten in response. Her lips barely moved as
she answered, "Just counting the minutes until I
don't have to be standing next to you."

"Me, too," he lied.

Wyatt didn't mind standing next to her. Morgan
amused him. She always had, once he'd gotten ac-
customed to the idea that she was a female who,
for reasons he couldn't quite fathom, was bent on
doing everything her older brothers did.

And there was no denying she was very easy on
the eyes. More now than ever before.

Or maybe, Wyatt mused as the priest finished
giving his instructions to the bride- and groom-to-

be, he'd just taken to noticing it more now that he was back.

With a marriage behind him to show him exactly what he didn't want in a woman, he had to admit that he enjoyed sparring with Morgan. He'd always appreciated quick wit, and he did like a woman with a sharp mind.

He slanted a look toward Morgan. Too bad that woman came with an ornery streak more than a mile wide.

Morgan could feel his eyes on her. His eyes and his criticism. Now what was he up to? She braced herself, knowing that sooner or later he was going to make some comment, some crack that would set her off. It was going to be a very long three weeks, she thought with an inward sigh.

One wedding up, three more to go, Morgan thought, adjusting the soft blue floor-length skirt of her hastily donned bridesmaid's dress. She cocked her head, critically giving herself the once-over in the full-length mirror to make sure she'd gotten all the buttons hooked on the long sleeves.

Not too bad, she decided, letting the skirt fall back into place.

She'd gotten through the rehearsal the other evening and the dinner that followed, the dinner Wyatt had treated them all to, with few battle scars. She was proud of the way she'd managed to behave. It helped to concentrate on all the happiness abounding in the room and not on the fact that Wyatt seemed to be always at her side.

Just like a lingering bad dream.

No, more like a reminder.

Morgan frowned as she stared into the mirror, recalling a summer's evening five years ago. An evening where the whole world had felt like it was crashing down on her twenty-year-old shoulders. Her father had just had a heart attack, and for twelve terrible, excruciatingly long hours, it had been touch-and-go.

Her whole family, as well as Wyatt and Casey, had gathered at the hospital, waiting, hoping, praying. She'd been the most vocal, rallying everyone, boosting their morale.

But underneath it all she'd been unable to handle the dreaded possibility that loomed over them like a dark cloud—the thought that the big, strong, strapping man she'd always turned to might not be there in the morning. Rather than let any of her family see her cry, Morgan had gone outside the hospital to walk around the grounds until she'd emptied herself of the last of her tears.

Wyatt had come looking for her that night. Why, she still didn't know. But he'd found her. Found, too, a vulnerable girl just barely a woman who needed, oh so desperately, to lean on someone. Because of the insanity of the moment, he'd been that someone. She'd resisted at first, because he was Wyatt and because she was embarrassed. But he'd been so kind, so understanding, that she broke down.

She'd poured out her heart to him that night, her heart and her fears and somewhere along the line, affections had gotten tangled up with all that. She'd never felt so strongly about anyone. Not before, not since.

Wyatt had listened to her so patiently, so kindly that she'd tried to lighten the charged moment with a silly comment. He'd laughed then, a warm, silky laugh that washed over and completely undid her at her moment of weakness. She'd never seen him like that. Sweet, patient, supportive and, yes, she would have even said, loving.

Wyatt had put his arm around her, and he'd held her when she'd suddenly begun to cry again. And then, when she'd looked up, she'd felt as if she'd never seen him before. Looked up and thought she saw a glimmer of her future in his eyes.

Just before he kissed her.

Just before she kissed him back.

Just before she'd made an absolute fool of herself, she thought angrily, her cheeks growing flushed as she remembered. She'd kissed him not as if he were Wyatt McCall, but as if he were…someone. Someone special. *Her* someone special.

Morgan shut her eyes for a moment, willing the sense of humiliation to recede. After all this time it was still there, lying in wait.

And then Wyatt had ruined the one moment they'd shared by holding her back at arm's length and telling her that he was engaged. To Judith Montgomery of all people. A walking, talking, brainless fashion doll.

To his credit, if he could be thought to have such a thing, he didn't try to add to the humiliation she already felt. As she remembered it, he'd almost sounded as if he regretted having to tell her.

Right, regretted it. She pressed her lips together as she slipped a headband of tiny white flowers into her hair. Regretted it only because he couldn't put the moves on her once she knew. As for his reasons for telling her, they hadn't been Simon pure, either. She was sure he'd only told her because he knew she would have cut out his heart had she found out about his engagement some other way, later, after she'd...

The possibilities of what might have happened that evening rose sharply in front of her to mock her.

Well, she hadn't made love with him, and that was all that mattered. The fact that she'd wanted to, that she'd suddenly been consumed with an overwhelming desire to make wild, passionate love with a man who had heretofore been the bane of her existence could just be chalked up to her bereft state of mind. She was just eternally thankful that Wyatt hadn't had the time or courage to take complete advantage of her vulnerable state.

Before she'd given Wyatt the verbal tongue-lashing he deserved, Quint had found and told them that Jake Cutler had taken a turn for the better.

So here she was, five years later, paired off with the man and required to look happy about it. Her frown deepened. Happy? Not hardly.

Squaring her shoulders, Morgan made her way out of the tiny room that had been set aside for the bridesmaids. Morgan's future sisters-in-law and Bridgette were gathered before the inner doors of the church. As always, she was the last one to arrive. This one time, she had really tried not to be. She'd timed everything perfectly, and then her heart had gotten the better of her and she'd stopped at Josh Miller's new home before leaving Butte. Stopped just the way she'd promised him she would.

There was no way she would have broken her word to him. Not when so many other people had already done that.

Morgan tried very hard to keep a professional distance between herself and the cases she handled as a social worker. Tried and usually failed to some degree. Even so, Josh was different. Orphaned a little more than six months ago, he was a brave little soldier who, despite his tender age, struggled not to be undone by the harsh world around him. She would have adopted him herself in a heartbeat if she were allowed.

But her hours were long, her schedule hectic, and she could only provide a single-parent home for a child who desperately needed a balanced life. Family Services frowned on the mere suggestion that she become his foster parent.

With all her heart, she hoped Josh was happy in the home he'd been placed in. All he needed was someone to love who loved him. Mentally she crossed her fingers for the four-year-old before she turned her attention to the wedding at hand.

"You do clean up really well, Cutler."

The teasing, deep male voice rippled along her skin. Morgan swung around to look at Wyatt, a quip ready.

The words melted on her lips, along with very nearly the rest of her.

No man had a legal right to look that good in a tuxedo, she thought, especially if he had a black heart. She'd stayed away from Wyatt's wedding, making up some excuse she no longer remembered, so the most formal attire she'd ever seen Wyatt wearing was a suit. He'd looked impressive enough in that. Seeing him like this was like getting hit with a twelve-torpedo assault from a U-boat.

"The same," she murmured as nonchalantly as she was able to muster, "can be said for you."

The compliment surprised Wyatt. He peered into her eyes, wondering if she was ill.

"Why, thank you, Morgan." He glanced toward

the closed doors. The strains of the wedding march were beginning and the doors were slowly opening. "Ready to launch your first brother on the sea of matrimony?"

She let out a sigh. "As ready as I'll ever be, I guess."

It was then that she realized he was holding flowers. Her flowers. A simple bouquet of pink carnations set amid a cushion of baby's breath. Wyatt presented them to her with a flourish that had her smiling against her will.

"The florist couldn't find you."

Morgan took the bouquet from him, waiting for him to say something about her breathless entrance. He didn't. "Thank you."

Wyatt offered her his arm. She looked at it for a moment as if she was weighing her options. There weren't any. Putting on her best face, she slipped her arm through his.

"I'll try not to drag my knuckles on the floor." He whispered the words softly against her ear, his mouth curving.

He would remember the comment. Morgan nodded, as if accepting the promise. "If you do, just remember that I'll be forced to step on them."

His laughter echoed in her head as they walked into the church.

The moment they entered, Morgan could feel her eyes beginning to sting. She blinked twice, determined to keep the tears at bay.

Unwilling to make an emotional spectacle of herself, she concentrated on the man walking next to her, hoping that would counteract any sentimental feelings wafting through her.

It didn't quite do the trick.

3

"God, I hope I look half that beautiful," Brianne leaned over and whispered to Morgan. Her wistful comment mingled with the strains of the wedding march vibrating along every available surface within the small, packed church.

Morgan stole a glance at the next Mrs. Cutler-to-be. By the look in Brianne's eyes, she was not only wistful, she was also itching for her camera. Morgan's lips curved into a smile. It was a camera that had brought Brianne into their lives. More specifically, into Kent's. She'd come to photograph a cowboy's life on a ranch for a magazine series and had fallen in love with her subject. For a moment, Morgan forgot her own emotions, stirred up to more than a fever pitch, as she listened to the eternal binding words being uttered.

As if someone who looked like Brianne would ever have to worry about her appearance. There were angels uglier than Brianne.

"You'll knock 'em dead and you know it," Morgan whispered back. Morgan's glance widened to take in Brianne, Denise and Ginny. "All three of you will."

And she, Morgan thought, she would be their bridesmaid. Every time. The eternal bridesmaid, marching slowly down the same aisle time and again, clutching a different bouquet, wearing a different gown, but with the same smile pasted to her lips.

Always a bridesmaid, never a bride.

It was a trite saying that suddenly held new meaning for Morgan and bothered her more than she was willing to let on, even to herself.

Though she knew she should be looking at her brother at this most precious of moments, Morgan found her gaze had somehow wandered toward Wyatt, entirely of its own, rebellious volition.

A shiver slid down her half-bare spine when she saw that he was looking directly at her.

Like a child caught with her hand in the cookie jar, Morgan squared her shoulders defiantly and looked straight ahead. Just in time to hear the priest ask for the wedding ring. Morgan watched as Will dug into his breast pocket and took out the eternal symbol of union. Hank's hand was trembling just the slightest bit as he held it out, waiting.

From her vantage point, Morgan would have been hard-pressed to say whose fault it was, whether the ring had fallen from Will's fingers or slipped from Hank's. But fall it did to the floor below with a little *plink,* landing on its side. As

Morgan and everyone else watched in fascinated distress, the ring rolled right between Will and Hank on the first leg of its odyssey down the center aisle.

Wyatt snapped to attention as the ring zipped by him. Chasing it down, Wyatt quickly covered the errant ring with his foot, halting its wanton getaway in mid-roll. Triumphant, he stooped down and picked the ring up, then held it aloft like a trophy.

He grinned at Hank as he handed the ring to him. "You're not getting out of this that easily, Hank."

The single breath that the wedding guests had been holding was released in a simultaneous wave of laughter that was instantly followed by a round of amused applause.

At least he was quick on his feet, Morgan thought. Or with them.

"Once again, repeat after me," the priest prompted when everyone had settled down. "With this ring—"

As she listened, the words seemed to echo in Morgan's head. She pressed her lips together, telling herself for the umpteenth time that she wasn't going to cry. She absolutely refused to. The cold that had peevishly chosen today of all days to descend on her was making her miserable enough already. She wasn't about to compound that effect and give herself a red nose by sobbing, the way her mother quietly was. Mothers were allowed to cry. They even looked radiant doing it. They were *supposed* to cry. Sisters, on the other hand, were supposed to cheer wildly when a sibling finally left the nest.

Morgan didn't much feel like cheering. But she would be damned if she was going to let anyone else know that.

She was, Morgan congratulated herself later, doing a hell of a job masking the way she felt. On the outside, she appeared overjoyed to finally see Hank abandon his wandering ways and settle down, especially with someone as sweet as Fiona.

As far as she could tell, everyone seemed to believe her. At times she actually believed herself.

But even at the reception back at the Shady Lady Ranch, amid the music, the dancing and the noise, the sadness within her, once rooted, insisted on growing. It was taking a larger and larger chunk of her as the minutes went by.

The situation wasn't remedied any by the fact that she had to share a first dance with Wyatt. She'd held off until the rest of the bridal party was on the dance floor. But then there had been no way around it. So, bracing herself for the bittersweet emotional gamut that lay ahead of her, Morgan allowed Wyatt to take her hand and lead her to join the others already on the floor.

He held her much too close for her comfort and

way too close for her peace of mind. When he leaned his cheek against her hair, she had to hold herself in check to keep from jumping.

If the woman in his arms were any stiffer, he could have gone diving off her. Wyatt drew his head back to look at Morgan as the music continued to envelop them. A hint of amusement shone in his eyes.

"Relax, Morgan," he prompted, "this is a celebration. You're supposed to be enjoying yourself."

Morgan raised her chin. "I will, once this dance is over."

Wyatt laughed. Morgan struggled not to allow the sound to filter through her. Her success was marginal. "Why Morgan, I'm crushed."

She hated when he laughed at her. Hated reacting to him this way even after all her lectures to herself. Morgan tossed her head and felt the flower headband dip slightly over her eye.

"Good."

With the tip of his finger, he slid the headband back into place for her. Morgan's breath hovered in her throat even though she told it not to. It irritated her that Wyatt appeared to know exactly what she was feeling—and that it amused him. It bothered her more that she was feeling it in the first place.

"You know," he commented softly against her

hair, "for someone who doesn't like to dance, you're very light on your feet."

Wyatt noticed how the fragrance she had on subtly drifted into his senses. He felt himself warming to it. How could he not, he wondered. It was sexy, exciting. Much like the woman wearing it.

Morgan felt as if she'd just finished running all the way from Butte to Serendipity. Damn it, she thought, why was her heart hammering like this?

"I didn't say I didn't like to dance, Wyatt. I just don't like dancing with you."

It would have sounded a great deal more convincing to Wyatt if her voice hadn't quavered at the end like that. "What do you say for one night, for Hank's sake, we set our differences aside?"

To the untrained ear, he sounded sincere, thoughtful. But Morgan knew better. He was a man who could take a woman's heart and break it without a second thought, cracking it like the shell of an egg and then tossing it aside without even realizing that it had been offered to him.

She should know.

Morgan raised and lowered her shoulder carelessly. "Fine with me."

To her surprise he crooked his finger beneath her chin and raised it until their eyes met. "Say it as if you mean it, Morgan."

She pulled her head away, afraid that if she didn't, she'd turn to mush right there in front of everyone. Just what she needed, to be publicly humiliated. "What do you want me to do, pinkie swear? Or would you rather draw my blood and become blood brothers?"

Why did he get the feeling that they had just crossed swords and that he was involved in a duel, the reason behind which he had no clue?

He shrugged nonchalantly. "You might as well draw yours, you've been drawing mine all day."

As if anything she said or did could have the slightest effect on him. "I haven't even left a mark on you," Morgan scoffed.

Maybe it was the twilight, Wyatt thought, with its soft promise of a star-filled sky. Maybe it was his best friend getting married and triggering all sorts of memories of things that he'd hoped for himself. Things that hadn't come to pass. Or maybe he was just damn tired of sparring with Morgan. He wasn't sure. He only knew that he didn't want to keep thrusting and parrying, not tonight.

"What have you got against me, Morgan?" Wyatt searched her eyes and saw no answer to the question.

Morgan knew she'd really let Hank's wedding get to her. Why else would she feel so terribly vulnerable? As if she'd melt against him if she had to go on being so close to him like this? Why couldn't she just remember how she felt when she'd all but offered herself to him on a silver platter only to discover that he was engaged to Judith?

"The night isn't long enough to tell you." She raised her head, listening. Relief came rushing up, hand in hand with regret. This wasn't a day she was going to forget soon. "Oh, look, the dance is over." She sighed. "I'm free." Disengaging her hand from his, she stepped back and sneezed at the same time. Her head felt as if it was going to explode.

Wyatt dug into his pocket and took out his handkerchief. He offered it to her.

Morgan eyed the handkerchief. It was immaculate. Was there someone doing his laundry for him? And who cared, anyway?

She arched an eyebrow. "Are you surrendering?"

For two cents.... Wyatt held onto his temper. "Just being polite."

Morgan swallowed a retort that had no place at her brother's wedding. Instead, she accepted the offering, stifling another sneeze.

"Thanks." She sniffled, then blew. There was a touch of mischief in her eyes as she looked at him. "I don't suppose you want it back."

He grinned at her. Patting her hand in his best patronizing manner, he closed her fingers around the handkerchief. "You sound as if you might need it again."

She didn't know if he was being thoughtful, or if, like a chimp banging at a keyboard and eventually pounding out a novel, it had come to him by accident. But Morgan knew she wasn't going to get a chance to find out. Miriam Lake had wiggled up behind Wyatt to snare his arm and his attention. Moving in like a woman with a mission, Miriam had placed herself between Morgan and Wyatt, and then pulled him onto the floor as another song began. If she remembered correctly, Miriam had belonged to the same cheerleading squad that Judith had. Why didn't that surprise her?

"Want to dance, Morgan?"

Turning, Morgan found herself looking up into Jared Adams's face. Jared was good-looking, successful and didn't have the annoying habit of contradicting everything she said. She had no idea why the prospect of dancing with him left her cold. And why dancing with Wyatt had done just the opposite. The medicine she'd taken just before the wedding for her cold had to be scrambling her brain.

"I'd love to." Morgan raised her voice loud enough to carry back to where Wyatt was dancing with Miriam. Glancing in their direction, she saw that her efforts had been wasted. They looked positively lost in each other. It figured.

As Jared's arms went around her, Morgan tried very hard to summon a modicum of excitement within her. She failed miserably. Jared came up short when measured, however involuntarily, against Wyatt. It annoyed the hell out of her.

* * *

"Dance with me, squirt. I haven't done my penance yet tonight."

Morgan didn't have to turn around to know that the entreaty belonged to Quint.

"That'll make two of us." She held up her hands, ready. "I haven't had my feet stepped on yet today."

She looked good tonight, Quint thought. Even better than usual. And there was a pink tinge to her cheeks, a flush that could only mean one thing outside of a sick bed. He'd seen who she'd been partnered with earlier.

He took her into his arms. "Saw you dancing with Wyatt."

Morgan raised her eyes to Quint's. It wasn't like him to tease her, not about Wyatt. He and Will usually left her alone on that subject. It was Hank, and sometimes Kent, who would yank her chain.

"Had to," she pointed out. "Tradition, remember?"

His smile began in his eyes before traveling down to his lips. He'd met his match in Ginny, now he wanted the same for his baby sister. Everyone should feel as good as he did tonight. "I remember a lot of things."

Her head felt like dampened cotton, thanks to the cold medication. She was in no mood to try to understand anything but the simplest of statements. "What's that supposed to mean?"

There was an edge in her voice. He didn't want

to start anything, not here. But he knew that Morgan knew exactly what he was alluding to.

"Nothing, I was just thinking that I can't really remember a day you and Wyatt weren't at it."

There was a reason for that. "That's because there aren't any."

Quint studied her for a moment, so intently that it unnerved her a little.

"Practicing your X-ray vision?" she finally asked.

He slowly shook his head. "Let me ask you about one thing I've always wondered, Morgan. Why is it that you're a reasonably complete, together, savvy lady until you get within spitting distance of Wyatt?"

Not him, too. She sighed. "The operative word would be *spitting*."

"There, that's exactly what I mean. What is it with you two?" His eyes narrowed, as if he were looking into her very soul. As if by doing so he ensured that she wouldn't lie to him. "Something going on between you that you're not telling the rest of us?"

Anger flashed in her eyes at the mere suggestion that she could number among Wyatt's dalliances. The next moment the anger subsided just as quickly. This was just Quint, looking after her the way he always did. He couldn't help the fact that it sometimes made him a pain.

Morgan forced herself to calm down. "No."

But Quint knew there had to be something more than she was saying. People didn't react the way Morgan did unless something had happened somewhere along the line to make them behave that way. He peered at her closely. Their lives had gotten busier these last few years. Had he missed something crucial?

"Did he hurt you somehow?"

He was all big brother now, and far closer to the truth than Morgan would have liked. "No man's ever hurt me, Quint."

He knew she wasn't that good at forgetting. "There was Blake."

Morgan pressed her lips together. Yes, there was Blake. Tall, dark, and, as it turned out, completely worthless. But not so's you'd notice at first, she thought. She'd launched herself into Blake's lair on an emotional rebound. The relationship, her longest, had lasted all of three months before she came to her senses.

Shrugging, she sighed. "Blake. Rhymes with mistake."

That's what they had all thought in the family. Quint had been the one to point it out to her. Not that his advice was wanted. "As I recall, you made that mistake right after Wyatt got married."

Morgan didn't care for the direction the conversation was going. She wanted the past in the past. All of it, Wyatt included. Looking for a way out,

Morgan spotted Ginny by one of the three banquet tables that had been set up.

"I see your lovely bride-to-be is looking lonely. Why don't you go and sweep her off her feet or pin a badge to her or—"

He'd intended to dance every dance with Ginny, but right now he was talking to Morgan. Or trying to. "I'll take care of Ginny, thanks." He pinned his sister with a look. "You're being evasive."

She let out a little hiss of impatience. "And you're pressing too hard. Let it go, Wyatt." She saw the grin bloom. "What?"

"You just called me Wyatt. Is there a reason for that?" Quint had his own theories about that.

There were times when her brothers were just too obstinate for their own good—or hers. "Yes. When I'm confronted with an annoying situation, naturally, I think 'Wyatt.'"

"Did I hear my name being taken in vain?"

Morgan stiffened at the sound of Wyatt's voice behind her and flashed an accusing look at Quint. He might have warned her. Turning around, her eyes swept dismissively over Wyatt.

"All of you is taken in vain, if you ask me, McCall." Then, to her dismay, she watched as Wyatt elbowed Quint out of the way. The latter looked more than happy to step back. "What are you doing?" she asked Wyatt.

Taking her hand, Wyatt arched an amused brow

at the stupidity of her question. "What does it look like I'm doing?"

She clenched her teeth together. "Looking to become a eunuch."

Wyatt had no idea why, but there was something fascinating about Morgan tonight. Something that kept reeling him in when he could be elsewhere, talking to someone else, dancing with someone else. Given a choice, he'd rather be here, having his head bitten off.

"No," he contradicted, "I'm cutting in."

It was past cutting in. She was already dancing away from Quint, who looked quite happy at the turn of events. Some help he was. She supposed that she could just walk away, but something kept her from doing that. She'd like to think that it was breeding.

"Don't I get something to say about this?"

Gallantly Wyatt nodded. "You get to say yes. Your partner's gone." Their hands joined, he used hers like an extension of his and indicated Quint behind her. Her brother was very busy brushing a kiss against Ginny's lips. "Now, unless you want to stand out here on the dance floor all by yourself, I suggest you dance with me. Smiling is optional."

He was doing it again, holding her against him so that she was in the middle of a hands-on anatomy lesson about the difference between men and women. Holding her so that her heart could have passed for a race car engine in the Indianapolis 500.

She had to get him to back away. "Breathing will be optional for you in a minute if you don't stop holding me like that."

But he didn't back away. If possible, he held her even closer. Morgan couldn't remember when she'd felt so alive. And so upset about it.

"Like what?"

Her eyes locked with his. "Like a farsighted tailor who's measuring me for a dress and has just lost his glasses."

The comparison tickled him. Laughing, Wyatt relinquished just a little of his hold. "Sorry, just a reflex."

Reflex her foot. He knew damn well what he was doing, and just how to do it. Still, she couldn't let him know that she was reacting to him. He'd never let her forget it.

"Is that how you hang on to all your women? By never letting them out of your grasp?"

He kept her hand tightly tucked within his and against his chest—just in case she felt like taking a swing at him. He put nothing past her. "No, just the ones I figure are dying to scratch my eyes out."

She laughed. So he could read her mind. "Large club, is it?"

Wyatt wasn't in the mood to talk about the women in his past. He'd come to the wedding alone, maybe for reasons he hadn't admitted to himself until now. "What about our truce?"

She tilted her face up to his. "I haven't killed you, have I?"

Did she have any idea how damn tempting she was? Of course she did, she was Morgan, the favorite, the indulged. Morgan, the woman who could break anyone's heart and just walk on by without even realizing what she'd done. She was as fickle as sunlight—and just as beautiful.

"And why," he asked softly, "would you want to do that?"

Was it her imagination, or were her knees getting watery? Maybe she shouldn't have had that second glass of wine, not when she was taking antihistamines for her cold.

She struggled to sound nonchalant. "General principle. Past wrongs. Future infractions. Why wait until the last minute?"

Wyatt had a feeling she liked him better than she let on. Just as he liked her better. Maybe tonight was the time to explore that, just this once. "You're all talk, Morgan, you know that? You just keep moving those pretty lips of yours, hoping to knock me over with the wind they create."

Pretty? Had he just called her pretty? Or was he just setting her up for a fall? Wouldn't be the first time, Morgan reminded herself. "I see you still have the same silver tongue."

Silver or not, Wyatt had an incredible urge to

run that tongue she was defaming over those lips of hers. The very thought excited him. But as he leaned into her, his mouth inches away from their goal, Morgan turned her head. And sneezed.

Spell broken, he struggled not to laugh at himself. He'd almost kissed Morgan. And probably came very close to having his lips ripped off. He ran a hand over the back of his neck. Talk about narrow escapes.

"You taking anything for that?"

What wasn't she taking for this, she thought sarcastically. "Dabbling in pharmacology are we now?" Maybe it was petty, but she didn't feel like going into any details whatsoever. Not with Wyatt. She'd gotten in trouble that one time for telling him too much. In trouble with herself. She had no intentions of it ever happening again.

Wyatt shrugged indifferently. "Just making conversation."

The indifference in his voice had her recoiling inwardly. It only served to remind her of the fool she'd once been. A fool over him.

"Well, don't trouble yourself." Breaking away, she went straight toward one of the waiters and plucked one of the wineglasses from his half-empty tray. It was her second.

Or maybe her third, she amended. She wasn't sure. What she was sure of was that she needed it right now to cut the bitter taste in her mouth. "I'll take one."

"That's your third, do you think you should?"

So he was keeping count, was he? Didn't he have anything better to do than haunt her? She took umbrage at his insinuation. "What are you doing, keeping tabs on me?"

Others ran for cover when her voice took that tone. Wyatt didn't budge. "Someone should, so you don't get into trouble."

She could feel a flush beginning in her cheeks. "McCall, you *are* trouble. You'd be the last one to keep me from it."

A smart man would have retreated by now, leaving her to suffer the consequences of her rash actions. But he didn't quite feel like being smart tonight. Not that she'd appreciate any of this.

"That's not going to go well with those cold tablets I saw you downing earlier." Then, very deliberately, he removed the offending glass from her hand.

She stared at him, astonished. Of all the gall. "Then why did you just ask me—"

"To see what you'd say." Just as he'd surmised, she was as scrappy, as argumentative as ever. "You're running true to form, Morgan. Except for those tears I see glistening in your eyes."

Damn it, leave it to Wyatt to notice. She blinked, willing her eyes to dry. "Those aren't tears, that's just an allergy."

Wyatt shook his head. Her excuse was all well

and good, except for one thing. "You don't have allergies."

Morgan frowned. What was this, verbal fencing? Or was he just trying to get her to lose her temper? "How would you know?"

"I know. I know a lot about you." The music began again, and he took her hand. When he began to dance, she followed. She didn't think not to. "Can't help but pick up things over the years, Morgan." The teasing tone left his voice. He could tell something larger was eating at her. "What's bothering you?"

"Other than you crowding my space?"

He inclined his head, indulging her. When all was said and done, he supposed he liked her, just like every other man in Serendipity. And probably Butte, too. But unlike every other man in Serendipity, he wasn't about to let her have her way. "Other than me crowding your space."

Morgan blew out a breath. Maybe she was feeling the alcohol, maybe it was the moment. Even as she formed the words, a small voice in her head was begging her not to, warning her of consequences.

For a second she paused to listen, then forged on ahead. "I don't want anything to change."

4

The minute the words were out of her mouth, Morgan knew she'd made a mistake.

Just like the last time.

She was sharing a feeling with Wyatt, something she'd sworn to herself she'd never do again. But though it cost her to admit it, there were times when that handsome face of his was actually easy to talk to.

You'd think she would have learned by now.

Abruptly, she walked off the dance floor again and headed back to the glass he'd taken out of her hand. Picking it up, she took a sip. It didn't help her forget that she'd slipped up.

Morgan bit her lower lip. She supposed that was how Wyatt had gotten his faithful following of loving females. He was not only drop-dead gorgeous, he was someone you found yourself opening up to in a moment of unexpected weakness.

CIA agents used that kind of talent to their advantage.

So did spiders, she thought grudgingly. The deadly kind.

Wyatt followed her, just as she knew he would. Morgan wound her fingers around the stem of the glass, not looking at his face. At the smirk she knew was most likely lingering on his lips. With her free hand she pressed the tips of her fingers against his lips to forestall any cryptic criticism coming from him and told herself that was *not* a shiver she felt shimmying down her spine.

"Before you say anything, I know it sounds childish, and I'm not trying for a Peter Pan thing here." She raised her eyes defiantly to his face, daring him to say anything. It surprised her to see that he wasn't laughing at her. Faced with unexpected kindness, she faltered. "It's…it's just that maybe the thought that things are never going to be the same again leaves me a little sad."

Damn, why had she just said that? He was only going to ridicule her.

But instead of making light of her feelings, Wyatt just shook his head. More gently than she thought possible, Wyatt removed her fingertips from his lips. "No."

She stared at him, completely confounded by the single word. "No?"

He smiled, more to himself than at her. Just now, with her eyebrows drawn together like that, he remembered the way Morgan had once been— a rebellious little girl who struggled so hard to be just like the big boys. She'd never realized that one day those big boys would all be vying for her attention.

"No, it doesn't sound childish," he elaborated. "And no, things are never going to be the same again, but it doesn't mean that you've lost anything."

She rolled her eyes. A lecture. Great, just what she didn't need or want. Served her right for letting her guard down. With a toss of her head, she drained the rest of the drink, then set the glass down. The next second, she felt a volley going off in her head as alcohol met medicine and initiated a hostile confrontation. It took her a second to refocus on the conversation.

"Right, I know, I've gained a sister." She didn't mean it to sound as nasty as it sounded. She loved Fiona and the others, she truly did. But she was momentarily mourning the death of childhood, and she didn't particularly care to be preached at.

"Yes, you've gained a sister, but I was going to point out that there are a host of possibilities that are just opening up for you."

She narrowed her eyes, trying very hard to find a light that made him look bad—and not like sin on toast. Had to be the lighting in here that was making him look so good to her. After all, he was still Wyatt. Nothing had changed, certainly not him.

Morgan fisted one hand on her hip. "Like?"

Wyatt had thought that would be evident to a woman as quick as Morgan. "Nieces and nephews to boss around."

She opened her mouth, then shut it again. What she was about to say didn't sound right, not in the light of the sympathy he was giving her. With a sigh, she studied him, trying to focus. She wished he'd stop getting better looking with each moment.

What was it about him that she found him so reprehensible, again?

Her head feeling just the slightest bit unsettled, she slid one hand along his collar. "If you don't stop being so nice, I'm going to have Quint haul you out of here as an impostor."

Wyatt caught her hand in his, lacing his fingers through it. Freeze framing her breath. "Then he'd have to haul both of us out. You're not exactly in character right now yourself, being sentimental like this."

Morgan shrugged in response. It had just taken him time, but he was obviously getting to the gloating part now.

Wyatt continued to peer at her face, trying to read her correctly. "Unless of course, it's that you don't relish the thought of having another female in the Cutler family." Morgan jerked her head up, her errant spirit returning in spades to her eyes. "Someone to steal your thunder."

As if that were possible, he added silently. If he said it aloud, he would have been going against type. Not to mention that she'd probably laugh her head off.

This was more like it, Morgan thought. He was being an annoying jackass again. How dare he suggest she was jealous of her brothers' fiancées?

"I'm not in the thunder business." Frost clung to her words.

Wyatt merely grinned at the denial. They both knew that she'd never be accused of being a shrinking violet. "Says you."

With a toss of her head, Morgan splayed her hand against his chest and all but moved him out of her path. "If you don't mind, it's getting a little stuffy here for me. I need some air."

With that, she made her way out of the house and onto the lawn. She didn't stop until she'd walked beyond the clearing and to the row of trees that bordered what her parents referred to as "the backyard." She had to move quickly to keep her heels from sinking into the ground and holding her fast.

Stopping by a tree, Morgan took a deep breath, then exhaled slowly.

She didn't need some air...she needed a lot of air, she thought, as her pulse began to slow down. And all of it away from him.

Morgan felt color creep up her cheeks, warming them. She slid her fingertips against her skin, as if to press the color back. What was wrong with her tonight?

Just having Wyatt standing beside her, looking down at her face, into her eyes, was eating up all the available pockets of air at an exceptionally rapid speed.

The Indian summer night, lush and pregnant with promise, wrapped moist fingers around her. Humidity had arrived like an uninvited guest to Hank and Fiona's wedding and seemed determined to linger until the last reveler left.

Morgan raised her hair away from the back of her neck, but there was no relief, no breeze to make it bearable. She hated humidity, hated heat. She was at her best in the winter, even when the wind brought the temperatures plunging down way below freezing. A hot night just wasn't her element.

Neither, apparently, was sparring with Wyatt, at least, not tonight.

Had to be the over-the-counter medication she was taking, Morgan thought, searching for an excuse why her pulse just refused to settle down. It was the medication that was making her all fuzzy.

Warm and fuzzy and thinking thoughts that had absolutely no business existing. At least, not about Wyatt.

Morgan sighed.

"You all right?"

Morgan bit her bottom lip hard to keep from shrieking. Damn, but he could sneak up on a person better than a mouse in soft-soled sneakers.

Wyatt had followed her out, concerned by the sudden pale cast on her face. It wouldn't be like Morgan to ask for help even if she were dying.

And it hadn't been like Morgan to share her feelings with him, either, now that he thought about it. The last time she had, he remembered, it had been just before he'd publicly announced his wedding.

Before he'd been *forced* to announce his wedding, Wyatt amended silently.

Not that Judith had held a gun to his head or anything to bring the marriage about. She'd merely told him of her condition, and his sense of honor and responsibility had done the rest.

At the time he'd thought it was the right thing. He supposed there was a little of the foolish optimist even in him. The right thing had turned out to be horribly wrong. For both of them.

And maybe, he thought, looking at Morgan, for more than just them.

But that was all in the past now. And he and Morgan were in the present.

Morgan nodded in reply to his question and instantly regretted it. Her head felt like it had just elected to go for a spin, leaving her body behind to fend for itself.

She didn't even fully realize that she'd gotten dizzy until she felt Wyatt's arms closing around her. Strong, hard arms that she almost sank into before her brain finally caught up to her.

Her body stiffened like the blade of a newly released jackknife. Morgan pushed against him, but he didn't release her immediately.

"Just what the hell do you think you are doing?" she demanded.

They were out of range of the house, but she could scream louder than anyone in the county if she had to. Morgan glared at Wyatt, waiting for an explanation. Or a reason to scream.

"Keeping you from getting grass stains on your bridesmaid dress. They tell me it's hell to get out." Wyatt released her. "Blue becomes you." The comment was delivered with all the feeling of a man taking note of the weather.

"Thank you," she mumbled, more dazed by the observation than by her momentarily reeling head. Morgan took a brief second to collect herself before she looked at him. "What are you doing out here? Why are you checking up on me?"

The woman would challenge an angel on a mission of mercy, not that anyone would ever accuse him of being an angel, Wyatt thought, amused at the notion.

"It's a dirty job, but someone has to do it."

Taking Morgan's chin in his hand, he turned her head toward the light from the lanterns that were strung up all around the perimeter and examined it. Her color looked as if it was returning. He should have known better than to be concerned about Morgan.

Seconds ticked by and she still hadn't drawn her head away. "If you're in the mood to play doctor…"

Their eyes met and held. Wyatt felt his pulse jump. Now there was a surprise. "Yes?"

The warm night seemed to envelop both of them. Morgan felt something twist within her. Something needy. "You picked a heck of an opportune time, but then, you're good at that."

The response surprised him more than Morgan could have hoped for even if she'd orchestrated this. He'd expected her to tell him to take a flying leap, not look up at him like that.

Like a woman who'd suddenly become aware of a deep-rooted longing.

Wishful thinking, that's all it was, Wyatt told himself. Wishful.

The single word echoed in his head, mocking him. Teasing him.

Yeah, he supposed he did like her at that, he realized again. More than liked her. But that route only promised trouble. Trouble by the truckload.

He'd never run from trouble before, and this certainly wasn't the night to start.

Feeling almost disembodied, Wyatt lowered his mouth down to hers until their lips just barely touched. All the while he kept waiting. Waiting for her to react, for the trap to snap, the rattler to strike, the jack-in-the-box to explode out of his tin home and laugh at him.

She surprised him more than any of those.

With a little moan, Morgan wrapped her arms around his neck and kissed him back. Kissed him as if there was an internal combustion engine housed within her tight, hard body and she'd just worked up a full head of steam, standing there in front of him.

The analogy bore more truth than he'd first thought, because if ever a man felt as if he'd just been run over by a train, it was him. A very long, very heavy train pulling about a million cars in its wake.

He'd always had a weakness for trains.

Blood churning, heating, Wyatt tightened his arms around Morgan, allowing himself, just for a moment, to go with his reaction before he began to entertain the very real thought of consequences.

And Morgan's retaliation.

But for now, all Wyatt wanted to do was feel. And enjoy.

He deepened the kiss. The madness increased, taking with it his sense of reality and whatever anchor had always kept him landlocked.

This was Morgan? Morgan Cutler? Wyatt found it all but impossible to believe that the woman in his arms, the woman who was very nearly sending him reeling off a cliff was the sharp-tongued female he'd crossed barbs with for the past fifteen years.

The last, and only, kiss they'd shared oh, so long ago paled in comparison to this.

For a woman whose words often stung bitterly, she tasted incredibly sweet. So sweet he knew he could easily be hooked on the taste of her mouth forever.

And therein lay his complete undoing.

He couldn't dwell on that now, not when every fiber of his body was begging him to take her, to make love with her now while the moment existed.

Slowly, as if he had no say in the matter, Wyatt began to glide his hands along her back, along her arms. Along her sides until his fingers slid over the tempting swell of her breasts. The more he touched, the more he tasted, the more he wanted.

He had to be out of his mind.

At that particular moment, Wyatt wouldn't have argued if anyone had said he was. He also knew he was going to pay dearly for this.

He didn't care.

Heat had spiraled through Morgan's core the instant she'd looked up into his eyes. The instant she'd known that he was going to kiss her. The instant the fear had materialized that perhaps he wouldn't.

Being Morgan, she'd jumped the gun. As always. She wouldn't have been Morgan if she hadn't. She'd always been the one to take the first step, push the first button, plunged headfirst into the first dare. She'd done all of that and more just now.

And gotten a hell of a lot more than she'd bargained for.

Every other time, anticipation, shimmering a moment before attainment, had always outshone reality. She had come to expect that. A real kiss was never as good as a phantom one. Reality was never as good as fantasy.

This time it was.

This time reality was beating in her chest like the wings of an eagle flying against the wind during a gale. Her breath hovered within her, not moving forward, not moving back, taking her to the point of explosion, and all because she'd felt Wyatt touch her. Felt him touch her and knew she wanted him to. Not just touch her, but have her. More than anything, Morgan desperately wanted to have him. Wanted to make wild, passionate love to him, here, on the land where she'd been born. The land she dearly loved.

She'd never been a cautious person. Any gray hairs her mother had all bore her name. But this time she was feeling utterly reckless.

And loving it.

Had to be the medicine. Or the wine. The wine, that was it. It was the wine. No, both. Why else was she behaving this way? Why else hadn't she stopped him?

Why else did she want him to go on?

Desperately the tiny part of her that could still think searched for a shred of a reason she could cling to once the madness passed and her blood cooled. She knew she was going to regret this, really regret this, but that would all come later.

For now, she wanted Wyatt to alleviate this craving, this hunger that was all but gnawing away at her.

She wanted to have something to regret later.

She was going to regret this. The words pounded in Wyatt's head even as he kissed her. Even as he lost himself in the taste, the feel, the scent of her. His conscience rubbed at him with the persistence of a pebble in a runner's shoe. He knew Morgan shouldn't have had the wine, not when she was taking something for her cold. And certainly not three glasses.

Damn it, why did he have to feel so responsible for her? Why couldn't he just enjoy her, enjoy the hands that were questing over him, all but ripping off his jacket? Enjoy this tigress who had emerged from beneath the guise of his best friend's sister.

Wyatt resigned himself. He was an idiot. There was no other name for him. But idiot or not, he couldn't take what she was offering. What he desperately wanted. Not when she wasn't fully responsible for her choice.

With an effort that would have made a superhero proud, Wyatt pulled away and caught her hands. If she only knew what this was costing him....

The confused question in her eyes almost tore him apart. And wouldn't she get a laugh out of that, out of knowing that at this moment, he probably would have bartered his immortal soul in exchange for making love with her.

His soul, but not hers.

He knew she couldn't be allowed to let this happen. Not when her mind was addled.

It took him a moment to find his voice and not sound as breathless, as strained as he felt. "I don't think you want to do this, Morgan."

Morgan froze. Translation—*he* didn't want to do this. He thought she was too tame, too boring to trifle with. Maybe he thought she couldn't knot her body into the positions his ex-wife could.

The realization that he was rejecting her while he had welcomed Judith echoed in her brain, threatening to make angry tears come. Morgan caught her breath like a diver plunging into icy water.

Summoning every last bit of dignity she could, she pulled her hands free of his and held them up, a rodeo rider who'd tied her calf up in record time waiting for the crowd to cheer. She had no idea how she forced the smug smile to her lips, but she did. Hurt pride could be a powerful thing.

"You're right, I don't." Morgan swept her eyes over him, all the while listening to her heart cracking. How could she have expected less? "I just wanted to see how far I could push you. Pretty far, apparently."

Turning her head away from him, she caught her lip, afraid if she didn't, the damning tears would flow freely on their own. Tears that belonged to a woman who knew when she'd been rejected. She might know, but she'd be damned if she'd let him know how she felt.

Cloaking herself in the bravado that was never far out of her reach, she raised her chin. "All right, now that I've had my fun for the evening, let's go back in."

He didn't want it to end like this. She'd reached him. Heaven help him, somehow she'd managed to reach him even after he'd been so sure that there was nothing left inside of him to touch. Not after Judith and her conniving ways.

Wyatt put his hand on her shoulder to draw her back. "Morgan, I—"

She shrugged him off as if he'd burned her. The smile, when it came, took effort and was in contrast to the frost in her eyes.

"You can stand out here and talk to yourself if you want, but I'm going back in." Stepping back, she kept a space between them. A large space. "Hank and Fiona are going to be leaving for their honeymoon, such as it is, at any minute and I don't want to miss seeing them off."

It really wasn't going to be much of a honeymoon. Three days at a bed-and-breakfast inn in

Monterey was all the time they could spare. The next weekend they had to return for Kent and Brianne's wedding. But Morgan knew that labels and places didn't matter. What mattered was being with the one you loved.

Something, she figured, she was never going to find out about. It seemed like a cruel twist of fate that the only one who could actually make her feel something for more than a moment was a man who would rather be with anyone else than her.

Not waiting for a comment, Morgan turned on her heels, a regal princess returning to her castle. She left Wyatt staring at her back.

Had he just imagined all this? One second she was hot enough to burst into flame, the next moment she could have been the iceberg that had broadsided the *Titanic*. Just what had gone on out here? It was for damn sure he didn't know.

With a sigh Wyatt began to walk back toward the house, keeping a good distance between himself and Morgan. It was safer that way. Up until now he'd always prided himself on being able to understand women, but it was a cinch that there was no understanding Morgan. There never had been. Like it or not, Morgan Cutler was in a category all her own.

He had a hunch she liked it that way.

As for him, he no longer knew what it was he liked, other than his sanity. Keeping it meant staying clear of Morgan from now on. He figured that wouldn't be all that difficult to do, not when she acted as if the plague was more desirable to be around than he was.

Looked like having a conscience was going to cost him, he mused, but maybe, in the long run, it was for the best. Morgan Cutler was more woman than he felt he could safely handle.

5

Wyatt had no idea why he couldn't listen to his own advice.

It was certainly simple enough—at least on the surface. He needed and intended to stay completely clear of Morgan. For all intents and purposes it seemed the only sensible thing to do. After all, she'd scrambled his brain, evaporated his resolve to keep from getting involved and then acted as if *he* had been the one who'd done something terrible.

Staying clear of her was the only option.

Following his own advice from Sunday through Thursday had been a piece of cake. Friday, however, was more like a pie in the face.

Still, Wyatt reasoned as he walked into St. Anne's Church for Kent and Brianne's wedding rehearsal, if he was serious about maintaining his sanity and not making a complete idiot of himself, it could be done.

At least in theory.

His body might be held captive by this uncalled-for onslaught of feelings and desires, but his mind could rise above all that and be elsewhere even at the most tempting of times.

His eyes slid toward Morgan.

Like that was possible.

She'd walked in a minute and a half after he had. As if she were hanging back the way he'd been trying to do, hoping to have everyone else already at the church so that there was a crowd to lose herself in.

Wyatt watched as Morgan moved down the aisle toward his pew, like a sleek jaguar out for the kill and scenting its prey.

First time he'd ever thought of himself in those terms, he realized. Prey equalled victim. He'd be damned if he was going to become hers.

Or worse, become one of Morgan's discards. Though he'd been gone for almost two years, he knew all about the men who sought her out. The men she dated and then disregarded as if they were some sort of batteries with an incredibly short shelf life.

He wasn't about to number among those.

Wyatt nodded at her as she took her place in the pew. He noticed that she sat down a little closer to the end than was necessary, given that they were the only two people in the row. The others had all filed in ahead of them, taking up the pews between theirs and the altar.

There didn't seem anywhere to go.

He could have had the entire expanse of Notre Dame Cathedral to move around in and still felt her presence. It was like being infected with a low-grade fever. It went with you no matter where you turned.

Morgan barely acknowledged his existence. Normally, that would have rolled off his back. He had no idea why tonight it stuck in his craw instead.

Maybe because she'd stuck in his mind all week, no matter what he'd done to blot thoughts of her out.

Wyatt turned his face toward the front of the church. He wasn't here to think about Morgan, he was here to rehearse another wedding. They were all here again, the same faces, but now the focus was on Kent and Brianne. Hank and Fiona had become the old married couple of the group.

And what had he become?

Damn frustrated, that's what.

What else could he be, not three feet away from Morgan and feeling that unscratchable itch taking hold of him? The itch that had very nearly gotten out of hand last Saturday.

The one he was paying dearly for not heeding. Served him right for trying to be noble. It was wasted on someone like Morgan.

Will turned around and glanced at his sister and Wyatt as Father Gannon was searching for a way to make his

words sound fresh and meaningful as he spoke to
Kent and Brianne. Will would've had to have been
dead not to notice that something was up. The tension coming from their pew was thick enough to
strangle anyone with even the most minor of res-
piratory difficulties.

At any moment, Will fully expected someone in
the choir loft to launch into a chorus of ''Dueling
Banjos.''

He began to rise, and Audra, Denise's six-year-
old daughter, caught his sleeve and looked at him
questioningly. ''Are you leaving?''

''I just want to see if everything's okay with
Aunt Morgan,'' he whispered to her.

His own wedding wasn't for another week yet,
but Will had already easily slipped into the habit
of referring to his siblings as Audra's aunt and un-
cles. He was looking forward to being her stepfa-
ther.

Almost as much as he was looking forward to
being Denise's husband.

''Oh.'' Audra released his sleeve. ''Okay.''

He brushed a kiss over her head. ''I love an
understanding woman.''

Audra covered her mouth with her hands as she
giggled.

Making his way to Morgan's pew, Will motioned for her to slide over.

Morgan remained rigidly where she was. To
move would mean having to sit that much closer

to Wyatt, and she was already as close as she intended to be. The man had insulted her, really insulted her, not once but twice. This last time was far more than she was willing to put up with. Never mind that she hadn't been in her right mind last Saturday. She had all but hurled herself at him, and he had neatly sidestepped her, allowing her to fall face first on the ground, humiliation draping over her like a dark, soul-staining shroud.

A woman didn't forget or forgive something like that easily.

Or ever, as far as Morgan was concerned.

"You can either sit down between us or talk standing up. I have no intentions of moving." Looking up at Will, Morgan's lips barely moved as she spoke.

Whatever this was, it was bad, Will thought.

"Something wrong between you two?" Will tried to keep his voice light. There was no use adding to the drama. "I mean, more than usual?"

She wasn't about to go pouring out her heart to anyone. Her brothers would probably laugh at the whole thing, anyway. Share a good joke with Wyatt. It wasn't as if this was something new. Only the hurt was.

"We're fine," Morgan ground out.

"Fine," Wyatt echoed after slanting a cursory look in her direction.

He was a hell of a long way off from feeling fine, but he wasn't about to say anything. The last thing he wanted was to give her the satisfaction of knowing that she'd been on his mind all week, resolutions to the contrary notwithstanding.

Will shrugged. It was useless to try to get either one of them to talk once they were in this mode. Even if he could, he knew it would be easier to get it out of Wyatt than Morgan, and for that he needed privacy. Maybe at the bachelor party tonight....

For a woman who was exceptionally vocal about her feelings, Morgan could still be exceedingly closemouthed when it came to something that was bothering her. Any way you cut it, Will thought, Morgan was a frustrating piece of goods.

A smile curved his lips. Having her in his life had prepared him for Denise, so he supposed he couldn't exactly be annoyed with his sister. If it weren't for Morgan, he would have said Denise was the most headstrong female in the world. It had taken some fancy talking on his part to get her to not only sell her carnival rides to Serendipity's town council but to stay on to help run the amusement park for which he'd drawn up the architectural plans.

Holding up his hands in mock surrender, Will began to back away. He'd find it all out in due time, he promised himself.

"As long as I know."

Wyatt waited until Will had left before turning toward Morgan. Maybe it would be smarter to keep his mouth shut and just muddle through this rehearsal and the wedding, but he'd never been much of a muddler. He wasn't one to just drift through life. He needed to take charge. Now was no different.

Inclining his head, he whispered, "Morgan, we have to talk," into her ear.

Shivers, delicious and hot, raced up and down her spine with no other goal in sight other than undermining her. She locked her shoulders rigidly.

"No we don't," she retorted crisply.

What was she doing, sitting here beside him? she wondered. She was just asking for trouble. She'd get one of the others to scoot over and make room for her.

Rising, she instantly felt his hand on her wrist. He'd touched her a thousand times before, yet this time, this time there was something different. *She* was different.

Morgan struggled not to make that obvious to him and shot him a warning look.

"Manhandling the groom's sister, particularly in church," she warned tersely, "is frowned on. You could get an extra century in hell for that."

He wasn't about to get beaten off by her sharp tongue. "I'd chance it if I thought it would do any good. About last Saturday—"

Oh, no, they weren't walking over that ground. Not when he'd made his disinterest so plainly known. Morgan looked right through him. "It was a lovely wedding, wasn't it?"

There was no way she hadn't been as affected by what had happened as he was. She hadn't been that out of her head. "You know what I mean."

Her eyes were steely as they regarded him. "Simple though you are, McCall, at times I *do* have trouble knowing what you mean. And this is one of those times."

With a jerk of her hand, she pulled free and moved into the aisle as her brothers and the others rose to begin the rehearsal. Morgan was counting on memory to get her through, because she hadn't heard a word Father Gannon had said since she'd walked in. Even if Will and Wyatt hadn't been talking to her, the pounding of her own heart would have blotted out the priest's words.

Kent placed the brimming pitcher of dark stout on the table in front of Wyatt in the booth. "Okay, what's going on with you and Morgan?"

Lost in thought, Wyatt looked up from his beer. For a moment he'd all but forgotten where he was. Serendipity's only bar had closed its doors to its walk-in clientele early this Friday night in order to give Kent the kind of royal send-off befitting a man of his previously confirmed bachelor state. The place was brimming to overflowing with cowboys, trail hands from the Shady Lady, which Kent managed, as well as men they had grown up with.

Normally the din and smoke, mingling with rousing music coming from the jukebox, would have been soothing to Wyatt.

But not tonight.

Nothing had been soothing to him, he thought darkly, taking another sip of his warm beer, since he'd kissed Morgan. The little witch had upended his world, and now she wouldn't even spare him two words. Telling himself it was better this way didn't do a damn thing for his disposition. It only agitated him further.

Because he didn't feel like talking about it, Wyatt shrugged in response. "Same-old same-old."

The hell it was. Kent found Wyatt's glib answer far from satisfying. There was nothing same about this. Even if Will hadn't pointed it out to him, he would have noticed that there was something going on between his sister and his friend, something different, more serious than usual.

As a rule, Kent didn't believe in meddling in other people's affairs. He didn't like having his own delved into, and he felt it only fair to return the favor. But life at home, and especially loving Brianne, had taught him that if you cared about people, you had unspoken permission to meddle in their lives. Even if they didn't like it.

Especially when you thought they were going down for the third time. If Quint hadn't meddled in his, he might have done the dumbest thing of his life and let Brianne walk out of it.

Not waiting for an invitation to join him, Kent made himself comfortable in the booth. "If that was the case, you wouldn't look as if you'd just eaten a barrel of rotten apples."

"What my inarticulate little brother is trying to say is that you're not your usual, easygoing self," Quint said as he slid in opposite Wyatt. He sensed rather than saw Kent nod his head.

"As a matter of fact," Will said, adding his two cents into the conversation and his body to the booth, "you look a lot like you did when you told us you were marrying Judith."

Will and his brothers were of the same opinion. They had all thought that was a black time in Wyatt's life, though they had all stood by him. Will had always suspected there was more to the union than Wyatt had told any of them.

"And how's that?"

The question came out of Wyatt's mouth in a sharp snap. He hadn't meant it to sound that way. Maybe they were right, Wyatt thought. Maybe he was too edgy. He drained his mug, then pulled the pitcher over and helped himself to more.

"Like you'd just taken part in your own execution," Hank elaborated. Because the booth was full, he pulled up a chair and straddled it. He planted himself directly in Wyatt's face. Something was bothering his best friend, and he wanted to know what. "So give, what's up?"

Confronted by all four Cutler brothers, Wyatt

felt a little overwhelmed. Having downed four beers didn't help, either. "Hey, what is this, an interrogation?"

"Nope." Quint eased his hat back with the tip of his thumb, studying Wyatt's face. The light hit his sheriff's badge and made it gleam. "If this were an interrogation, you'd know it, boy. This is just a little friendly interest coming from your friends." He raised a brow. "Anything going on between you and Morgan we should know about?"

Quint had a feeling he already had the answer to that, but he wanted to hear it from one of the two parties involved. It was easier trying to corner Wyatt on the subject than Morgan.

A shadow fell over the table. "Any of you boys ever consider the fact that Morgan's a big girl now, entitled to her privacy? And that she doesn't need her big brothers pushing their even bigger noses into things that don't concern them?"

"Uh-oh, this doesn't sound good." Quint didn't have to turn around to know that Morgan had crashed the party and was standing behind them. Talk about timing. "Who let you in, squirt? This is a private party."

It took effort on Morgan's part not to wince at the nickname he'd used when she was little. She knew that there was nothing but affection behind it, as well as behind her brothers ganging up on Wyatt to pump him. But affection or not, some things about her life were not up for public display.

Her accusing glance swept over all of them. "Not that it matters, but I bribed the bartender. And don't change the subject—"

But changing the subject was exactly what Quint aimed to do. He was in no mood for a burst of temper from his little sister.

"This is a bachelor party, Morgan." He deliberately slid his thumb along his badge, silently reminding her that he was the sheriff as well as her brother. "There're no women allowed."

Morgan hated when Quint started being a stickler. She knew he was just trying to tease her, but her tolerance had done a vanishing act in the past week.

Annoyed, Morgan waved a disparaging hand at the woman who had popped out of an oversize cake in an undersize bathing suit less than an hour earlier. "*She's* here."

Quint kept a poker face. "She's entertainment."

"Yeah, entertainment." Kent's eyes were dancing.

"You keep quiet or I'll tell Brianne on you," Morgan warned. She shifted her attention back to Quint. "I can be entertainment." Her lips curved. "Want me to sing?"

Kent winced while Hank covered his ears. Morgan was easy on the eyes, but they were all agreed that her singing made cats run for cover. "Oh, God, anything but that."

Quint was already on his feet, nodding toward

the bar. "Suddenly I feel a thirst for something stronger than beer coming on." He looked from one brother to another. "Why don't you all join me?" But when Wyatt began to slide out, ready to follow the others to the scarred mahogany bar, Quint clamped a restraining hand on his shoulder. "Not you, Wyatt." He didn't bother hiding his amusement as he looked at Morgan, then Wyatt. "You two have things to iron out."

Morgan was really getting tired of her brother thinking he could run her life just because there were times Quint was more levelheaded than she was. "No we don't—"

Quint fixed Morgan with a pointed look. "You want to stay? Iron." The subject wasn't up for debate.

Morgan let out a long, slow breath as her brothers all went to the bar. She loved them, but there were times she really would have relished pummeling all of them to the ground. Too bad she wasn't ten anymore. Adulthood had its drawbacks.

She thought of last Saturday and the way Wyatt had made her feel for a very precious moment. And the ache and frustration that came immediately after. Yeah, adulthood certainly had its drawbacks.

Wyatt couldn't remember ever being uneasy in Morgan's presence. Uncertain, maybe, about what she had up her sleeve, but never uneasy. How the hell had he turned that corner? She was still Hank's little sister, still a royal pain in the neck…but there was more and he knew it. And the ground between here and there was all quicksand with nothing to mark the thin, narrow path that was safe for him to tread.

Maybe there wasn't a safe path.

Wyatt held up the pitcher of beer. "Want a beer? It's a little warm." He liked it that way, but he knew most people didn't.

Resigned, Morgan sat down. She shrugged indifferently at his question. Since she was here, she might as well have a beer. Anything to cut the dryness in her throat.

She picked up an empty mug one of her brothers had left behind and held it out to Wyatt. "I don't mind. I'm not hard to please."

Wyatt almost choked. "Yeah, right." He poured the dark liquid carefully. When Morgan began to move the mug aside, he caught her hand and held it in place until he was finished. "Have you looked under the words *prima donna* in the dictionary lately? They have your picture. Damn good likeness, too."

The foam rose quickly and spilled over the side, christening her fingers. Without thinking, Morgan slipped her fingers into her mouth. Watching her, something twisted in Wyatt's gut. The ache in his forearm reminded him he was still holding the pitcher aloft. He set it down.

"What are you doing here, anyway?"

Morgan wrapped her hands around the mug. What was she doing here? The question echoed in her head. She honestly wasn't sure anymore. Maybe it was that same quirky feeling that had elicited sadness from her every time she thought of her brothers' weddings.

She tried to seem blasé as she said, "I wanted to see what a bachelor party was like. Figured after this month, I'd never get a chance." Morgan tipped back her mug. The dark beer slid down easily enough, but it did nothing to quench her thirst.

Wyatt laughed and raised his glass to her. There was only one Morgan Cutler, thank God. "You've got guts, I'll give you that, Morgan. No other woman I know of would come waltzing into a bachelor party."

She took it as a criticism and knew she shouldn't. Funny how when he said the moon was yellow, she wanted to say it was green. She glanced toward the other woman in the bar who was whispering something into her cousin Carly's ear. She could see color rise in Carly's cheek. Even though he was in his twenties, Carly still had a sweet innocence to him.

"You mean you're not acquainted with her?" Morgan asked.

Leaning against his seat, Wyatt raised his eyes innocently to Morgan's face. "Who?"

"Don't give me that innocent look, McCall. You stopped being innocent two minutes after you were born, right after you propositioned your first nurse.'' She took another long swallow of her drink. ''I'm referring to the little number in the even littler outfit.'' She wasn't aware of frowning, but Wyatt noted it. ''The one giving you the eye.''

Wyatt didn't bother turning around to look at the other woman. Like Will said, she was the entertainment and he hadn't felt much like being entertained tonight. He'd come to the party because this was for Kent, and his sense of attachment to the Cutlers forbade him sending his regrets in his place.

Besides, he'd thought that a little socializing might make him forget the events of last weekend. That certainly had backfired in his face.

Wyatt finished off his beer and set the mug down. ''Never saw her before in my life.''

Morgan had no idea why she pressed. She couldn't care less what he did in his free time. But the question still came out. ''Is that what you say about every woman after you've had your fill of her?''

His eyes locked with hers. ''Morgan, what is it you want from me?''

She couldn't answer that. Couldn't answer because she didn't know. Frustrated, angry, she rose, an arrow without a target.

''Simple.'' She looked down into his face. ''I want you to die. Just don't do it at any of my brothers' weddings.''

It seemed to Wyatt that he was constantly watching Morgan walk away from him. It didn't do much to improve his mood.

"What are you smiling about, old man?"

With loving hands, Zoe brushed a hair from her husband's lapel. Maybe she was prejudiced, she thought, but he was the handsomest man at the reception. All these years and he could still set her heart fluttering. Ever the gracious hostess, she'd been weaving in and out between her guests when she'd looked up and seen his pleased expression clear across the room. It had all but beamed and flashed. She'd felt compelled to ask after its source. There was more involved here than just being the proud father of the groom. She knew her man.

She read him like a book, Jake thought, grateful he'd never had call to keep things from her. He knew it'd be a losing battle. "Oh, I just decided to give nature a little shove."

The comment made no sense to her. "Have you been drinking?"

Teasing, she pretended to sniff his breath, but she knew Jake better than that. Her husband had restricted himself ever since the heart attack that had frightened them all. If he imbibed at all, it was very minimally. It annoyed him some to be so careful, but she knew he valued those he loved too much to ever put them through hell again.

She'd inadvertently stumbled on a connection,

Play The *Lucky Hearts* Game

and get...
FREE BOOKS, a FREE GIFT...
and MUCH more!

Yes! I have scratched off the silver card. Please send me my **2 FREE BOOKS** and **FREE MYSTERY GIFT**. I understand that I am under no obligation to purchase any books as explained on the back of this card.

Scratch Here!
then look below to see what your cards get you...

301 SDL CNGL   **201 SDL CNGK**

Name _____
(PLEASE PRINT)
Address _____ Apt.#

City _____ State/Prov. _____ Zip/Postal Code _____

Twenty-one gets you
2 FREE BOOKS and a
FREE MYSTERY GIFT!

Twenty gets you
2 FREE BOOKS!

Nineteen gets you
1 FREE BOOK!

TRY AGAIN!

Offer limited to one per household and not valid to current Silhouette Yours Truly® subscribers. All orders subject to approval.

PRINTED IN U.S.A.

DETACH AND MAIL CARD TODAY!

© 1998 HARLEQUIN ENTERPRISES, LTD. ® and TM are trademarks owned by Harlequin Books S.A., used under license

The Silhouette Reader Service® — Here's how it works:

Accepting your 2 free books and mystery gift places you under no obligation to buy anything. You may keep the books and gift and return the shipping statement marked "cancel." If you do not cancel, about a month later we'll send you 4 additional novels and bill you just $2.90 each in the U.S., or $3.24 in Canada, plus 25¢ delivery per book and applicable taxes if any.* That's the complete price and — compared to the cover price of $3.50 in the U.S. and $3.99 in Canada — it's quite a bargain! You may cancel at any time, but if you choose to continue, every other month we'll send you 4 more books, which you may either purchase at the discount price or return to us and cancel your subscription.

*Terms and prices subject to change without notice. Sales tax applicable in N.Y. Canadian residents will be charged applicable provincial taxes and GST.

If offer card is missing write to: Silhouette Reader Service, 3010 Walden Ave., P.O. Box 1867, Buffalo NY 14240-1867

BUSINESS REPLY MAIL

FIRST-CLASS MAIL PERMIT NO. 717 BUFFALO, NY

POSTAGE WILL BE PAID BY ADDRESSEE

SILHOUETTE READER SERVICE
3010 WALDEN AVE
PO BOX 1867
BUFFALO NY 14240-9952

NO POSTAGE
NECESSARY
IF MAILED
IN THE
UNITED STATES

Jake thought. "No, but I did send two certain people down into the wine cellar for some more wine—separately of course." He winked broadly at Zoe.

Zoe glanced around the room, but she had little need to. She could guess. "Morgan and Wyatt?"

Jake grinned. "None other."

Zoe wondered if perhaps his well-meaning action might have the opposite effect and push the two farther apart. "Maybe you shouldn't have interfered. They'll find their own way."

Jake's grin broadened as he slipped an arm around her shoulders. He thought of the cellar. And the light bulb he'd purposely removed from one of the three overhead fixtures scattered through the area. It could be downright romantic down there. He and Zoe had found it that way years ago.

"That's what I'm counting on, Zoe. That's what I'm counting on."

Zoe laughed, shaking her head. Her husband liked to think of himself as being tough as nails, but he was a romantic through and through. "You just like attending weddings."

His laugh boomed. "Hell, yes. And getting them all out of the way one after the other is surely a good idea. Get those grandkids started coming." He looked around, picking out his sons before looking down at his wife again. "We surely did turn out a handsome bunch of kids, didn't we, Zoe?"

Zoe placed her hand on his chest and sighed. Life had been very, very good to her. Most of it, until the last ten years, had been spent pinching pennies and trying to get by, but by her count, she was far richer than most women.

"That we did, Jake." Zoe looked over to where Kent and Brianne were standing by the banquet table. Resplendent in wedding finery, they made a striking couple. Her mother's heart welled up, as did her eyes. "That we surely did," she whispered.

Jake looked at her. "You're not going to cry again, are you?"

Zoe sniffed. "No."

He handed her his handkerchief, tightening his other arm around her shoulders. "I didn't think so."

6

The darkness beneath her feet assaulted her like a misshapen monster, born of the unknown, the moment Morgan walked into the cellar. Instinctively her hand tightened on the banister as she flipped on the light switch before taking a single step.

The bulb flickered weakly, warning of its imminent demise.

Morgan had never liked the wine cellar.

Silly though it seemed, the uneasy feeling hovering over her was a holdover from early childhood. She'd been about six or seven when she had gone down to the cellar alone on a dare from Quint, Hank and Kent. She could still remember the way her heart had pounded in her chest, the way it had echoed in her ears. But even at that age, she had refused to let any of her brothers know that the mere mention of the cellar caused her to break out in a cold sweat. Her young imagination went into overdrive whenever she contemplated the kinds of creatures that hid there in the murky dark.

Her imagination had been just what her brothers were banking on. They'd rigged a long, thin, white sheet-shrouded figure to come flying out at her, just as she crossed the floor to the wine racks. Her small foot tripped a wire, the sheet covered "ghost" came charging out at her and she had run out, shrieking at the top of her lungs.

Quint, Kent and Hank had fallen over, their sides shaking hard with laughter. But they hadn't laughed as hard when she'd launched herself at all three of them, pummeling them with her small fists. It had been Will who had finally pulled her off them, after giving her a minute or two to vent. He told her later he figured she'd earned it.

She wished Will was here now, getting the bottle of wine her father wanted instead of her. That tiny pinprick of fear that had been born that long-ago day still hovered over her.

The cellar ran the length of the house, but because of structural reasons Will had explained, it was L-shaped. The first part was taken over for storage, leaving the wine racks to be housed at the rear of the cellar.

She had to cross the whole of it to get there.

The light from the single bulb at this end added to rather than subtracted from the nervous feeling skittering through her.

Stupid way for a woman in her twenties to feel, Morgan thought.

The feeling refused to fade away. Just like other feelings refused to leave no matter how much she prodded them to go.

A noise coming from the rear of the cellar startled her. Morgan froze instantly, straining to listen, straining to see. But the light at the rear of the cellar was just as dim as in the first section. More noise.

The clinking sound of wine bottles being moved echoed through the cellar. It was a ghostly noise.

The next moment she saw a figure emerge from the shadows. Her breath caught in her throat, threatening to strangle her. Instinct rather than conscious thought had Morgan darting behind an unstable tower made up of old boxes that housed even older memories. For a moment, she was six again, hearing nothing but the pounding of her own heart.

And then there was something else. The sound of bottles being set down. The sound of soft footsteps on the cement floor. Approaching.

The second Morgan felt the hand on her shoulder, she swung around and charged, throwing her full weight forward against whoever or whatever was there in the cellar with her.

Toppling down on top of her would-be assailant was a move that definitely hadn't been in her plans.

The wind completely knocked out of her, Morgan struggled to draw a breath. The scent of the cologne told her the story even before she focused her eyes in the semidarkness.

The so-called assailant she'd tackled, the one she was now smack-dab on top of, was Wyatt.

The next minute, as indignation neatly replaced fear, Morgan felt Wyatt's arms close around her. Wiggling did not help the situation. Morgan resorted to a heavy doze of temper.

"What are you doing, following me?" she demanded.

If it occurred to Wyatt that this was an awkward way to carry on a conversation and an even more awkward way to conduct an interrogation, he didn't show it.

What he showed, to her increased annoyance, was amusement. She hated it when he got that look in his eyes, the one that made him out to be superior to her.

"Following you? How can I be following you when I was here first?"

Morgan was in no mood for logic. She was having too much trouble clinging to anger. It was breaking up like a wet tissue in a whirlpool. Something else was going on within her.

"Don't try to twist things around," she warned, struggling to draw away. "And let me up."

He gave no indication that he was about to do anything of the sort. Not yet. Wyatt was having too good a time baiting her. And enjoying her.

"Hey, you jumped me, not the other way around, remember?" His eyes teased hers just as much as his body did. More. "Now I'm not letting you up until you explain yourself."

This wasn't heat she was feeling flooding her, and it certainly wasn't desire. It *wasn't*. Morgan felt herself losing the internal argument she was waging.

"Explain what? I came down here, heard a noise and then you put your paw on my shoulder." She realized that she sounded breathless. Morgan struggled for composure. "I had to defend myself."

He took exception to her calling his hands paws. "Hey, I play piano with these." He released her long enough to hold up one hand in front of her before returning it to its present duty—holding her against him. "They're not paws. And I just wanted to know why you followed me down here."

Color bloomed in her cheeks. "I did *not* follow you down here. I had no idea you were here at all—" Her eyes narrowed as the lie he'd just said echoed in her brain. "And you do not play the piano." Mastering the piano seemed far too sensitive an accomplishment for a man as irritating, as callous as Wyatt.

He had no idea why the smug look on her face tickled him. Why everything about her just kept drawing him in like some poor fish that had no say in his fate. He had every say in his fate.

And yet…

God, but she felt good like this. He shifted ever so slightly and saw something bloom in her eyes. ''Five years of lessons and hideously long practice sessions say you're wrong.''

She pinned him verbally. ''If you play the piano, why didn't Hank say something?''

There was a good reason for that, Wyatt thought. ''It wasn't something I broadcasted.'' He saw she still didn't believe him. It really didn't matter. But he still said, ''Some things a man likes to keep to himself.''

What he wasn't keeping to himself, he realized, was his reaction to her, to having her splayed out like this across his body. Apparently a stiff upper lip wasn't the only thing he was keeping about the feelings Morgan was stirring within him.

Damn it, why did it have to be her? Of all the women he knew, why was Morgan the one who made him feel like this?

Morgan's eyes widened as she suddenly realized that she was still lying on top of Wyatt. And had stopped making an effort to get up. Well, that could be remedied fast enough.

But as she began to rise, Wyatt moved his hands from her waist to her face, immobilizing her. He framed her face with his palms. The touch was light, barely even registering, yet it held her as fast as a sliver of iron was held fast by a magnet.

''What other things are you keeping to yourself?'' Morgan heard herself whispering.

Instead of answering, Wyatt dove his hands into her hair and brought her mouth down to his. "You talk too much, Morgan."

The protest she was about to offer died before it reached her lips. Snuffed out by a wave of feelings so strong, it left nothing in its wake. Nothing but more feelings.

Feelings ravaged her body as the first kiss flowered into another and then another, each one longer, deeper, more passionate than the last until finally, all the differences between them fell away and their very souls seemed to merge.

It was like a revelation. Suddenly Morgan couldn't get enough of him, couldn't get enough of the sensation that was climbing through her. Like a resonant echo, it rushed from place to place within her, rattling the very foundations of her life.

Rather than challenge it, she was desperate to hang on to it as long as possible.

She felt his hands race along her body, felt her own fingers tremble as she did the same. Banishing all thought, all common sense, Morgan fumbled with the buttons on his shirt, frantically pushed first a jacket, then his shirt off his shoulders. Unable and unwilling to recognize herself, she tugged on his waistband, completely conscious that as she divested him of his clothing, he was doing the same with hers.

And that she wanted him to.

The fire climbed.

It didn't matter than they were on the floor of her parents' cellar, didn't matter that there were several hundred people one floor above them, any one of whom could come looking for them at any second. Didn't matter that she'd made herself promises that she'd sworn she would die before breaking.

None of that mattered.

The only thing that mattered to her at this moment was that she be allowed to grasp the pinnacle of pleasure that flashed and gleamed just ahead of her. Just a breath out of reach.

She'd never felt this kind of excitement, never known this kind of desire. It was as if she was completely convinced that she was going to die if he didn't make love with her. This moment. Now.

This time, she wouldn't let him back away. Not if either one of them were to live out the night.

Somewhere, far in the recesses of his mind, Wyatt knew he should stop himself. It was up to him to say no. His responsibility. It was no more right tonight than it had been a week ago. Even though there were no cold medicines, no glasses of wine to blame this on, it still didn't make what was happening right. She was his best friend's sister, not some tumble in the back seat of a car to be enjoyed the way he had done once when he was young and dumb and didn't know any better.

He knew better now and whatever he said to the contrary, he didn't want to hurt Morgan.

And didn't want to be hurt by Morgan.

But her skin felt like warm silk and her mouth was heated sin and he had an overwhelming weakness and desire for both. A warehouse of lectures couldn't force him to stop, to abandon the path he found himself on.

He had no choice in the matter.

Not when there was this madness rushing around in his veins, not when his body pulsed and throbbed, demands wracking it.

Not when she tasted sweeter than any known substance on earth.

Always proud of knowing where he was at any given moment, Wyatt realized that he'd lost his way. And lost himself in her.

It was all a haze, yet somehow every single part was oddly crystal clear to Morgan. Every kiss an imprint, every touch a torch that continually ignited her, building the flame within her even higher.

When their bodies finally joined, when relief and excitement finally exploded, leaving contentment to slowly drizzle down over her like a soothing rain, Morgan felt so completely spent that breathing was an effort. Breathing evenly was out of the question. Her heart was racing faster than the speed of light, and she doubted if it would ever slow down.

And knew beyond a shadow of a doubt that she would never be the same again.

But even as the afterglow clung to her body like a fine mist, reality began to rebuild a toehold.

Morgan turned her head toward Wyatt. Their eyes met and held. The glow receded. Morgan drew in her breath, feeling it rattle jaggedly in her chest.

What the hell had she just gone and done? How could she have allowed herself to become one of Wyatt's legion of women? Where was her pride? Her honor? Her brains, for heaven's sake?

The questions throbbed in her head almost as insistently as her desire had half an eternity ago. Morgan wanted to shriek just as loudly as she had that time her brothers had launched the ghost at her. To shriek and run away as fast as she could.

Instead, she pulled herself together like a queen under siege by the enemy and raised her head, her eyes reduced to twin stilettos as they bore into Wyatt.

"If you ever, *ever* breathe a word of this to anyone," she warned, enunciating each word slowly, "I'll cut your heart out."

"Threat duly noted," he replied glibly.

Nodding, he rose and extended his hand to Morgan. To his surprise, she took it. He gently drew her up to her feet.

Quickly, their backs to each other, they got dressed in an awkward, heated, tense silence.

Finished, Wyatt turned toward her again. He couldn't just let it go like this. Something had to be said, something had to be understood, although what it was he didn't know, since he hadn't a clue as to what he was feeling right now.

Still, he'd never just made love to a woman and then walked away. It wasn't the way things were done.

"Morgan—"

The last thing Morgan wanted right now was the sound of his voice. If he was going to laugh or apologize or even just breathe, she might not be responsible for her reaction.

"I don't want to talk about it," she said tersely. There was no excuse for what had just happened, but she offered up one, anyway, more for herself than for him. "I haven't been myself lately."

The hell she hadn't, Wyatt thought. She'd been more herself than ever. There was a fire and a passion about the way she made love that branded what had just happened. And spoiled him for anyone else, he realized suddenly. "That would explain the pleasure, then."

She looked at him sharply. Was he going to gloat? "Whose?"

He wasn't in the mood to fight. Tease, maybe, but not fight. Not just now. "Mine," he allowed freely. "Yours maybe."

She shrugged, trying to be as nonchalant as she didn't feel. "It was all right."

She sounded as if she were reviewing a third rate movie. He knew better. It wasn't his pride, but the feel of the woman beneath him earlier that told him what she felt.

His mouth twitched. "I'll try not to get a swelled head."

She supposed he deserved better. "All right, it was more than all right." She'd be damned before she admitted that the very earth had moved, moved so much that she lost her bearings as to which was the sky and which was the ground. "What do you want me to say?"

He didn't need accolades. One small admission was all he was after.

"That'll do fine." He bent down and picked up the flowered band that had fallen from her hair. Instead of giving it to her, he slid it slowly into place. "But what I'd like you to say is why."

She touched the band, as if to assure herself that he had placed it correctly. She could feel her heart begin to speed up again. She wished he wouldn't look at her that way. Wouldn't touch her like that. "Why what?"

His eyes lingered on her lips. "Why did you make love with me?"

With, he'd said *with,* not *to.* And that was the difference, she realized. However insane, it had been a mutual act. An act she'd wanted to have go on forever.

She had to be losing her mind.

Morgan covered her face with her hands. What was she going to do? The one time she actually felt something wondrous, and it had to be with the one man on earth she didn't want to feel anything for. The one man in the world who would take great pleasure in flexing his sexual muscles and then just walking away from her.

"Well?" he asked, still waiting for an answer.

"Why did I make love with you?" Morgan repeated the question, stalling for time as she tried to sound amused. "You caught me off guard," she finally said.

It was a crock and she knew it and she knew that he knew it as well. "Is that how you react when you're caught off guard?"

She knew it. He was laughing at her. He'd probably laugh about this, once he had the chance to. The way he'd probably laughed when she'd kissed him in the hospital parking lot in the rain five years ago.

"You jumped my bones before I had a chance to push you away."

As if anyone could ever "get the jump" on Morgan unless she wanted them to. Wyatt cocked his head, looking at her. "Who jumped whose bones?"

Her eyes widened. Was he going to somehow turn this around so that it sounded as if she'd stalked him? "I did not jump your bones, I was defending myself."

Wyatt laughed. "How? By 'loving' me to

death? That'll make a hell of a new page in the self-defense manual.''

She glared at him. Why was it that he made her tongue tangle like this? Did he enjoy humiliating her? "You're impossible."

Unable to resist, he slid the back of his hand along her cheek. This had to be one of heaven's little jokes, to stir him this way about a perverse woman who hated his guts. "No, I think you just learned that I'm not. I can be had."

All she wanted to do was get away. And all she could think about was the way his mouth had felt on hers. She had to be going crazy. "It happened, all right? Don't make anything more of this than it was."

"All right." Wyatt inclined his head obligingly. "And you do the same."

Morgan picked up the first bottle she could lay her hands on. Her father, after all, was waiting. "I'm not making anything out of this at all. This isn't even a footnote in my life."

He smiled. She was certainly more than a footnote in his. "Then someday, Morgan, I'd love to get my hands on your bibliography."

Whirling on her heel, her eyes flashed a dark blue as she looked at him. "You leave my 'bibliography' out of this, McCall. And while you're at it, leave me alone, too."

That would be, Wyatt thought, the best for both of them. "Whatever you want, Morgan."

But somehow, he had a feeling that his conscience wasn't going to let him follow that course.

What she wanted, Morgan thought as she hurried out of the cellar and up the wooden stairs, was for the last forty-five minutes or so to have never happened.

More than that, for Wyatt McCall to have never come back into her life.

By the time she'd reached the top of the stairs, Morgan felt she'd reasonably collected herself. At least her clothes, if not her soul, were back in order. The latter might never be again.

With a toss of her head, she crossed the large room where the reception was being held and walked up to her father.

"I believe you asked for wine." Primly Morgan handed her father the bottle she had picked up from the floor.

She stiffened as Wyatt brushed by her with his own offering. He held it out to Jake.

"Ditto." A bemused expression played on Wyatt's lips as he studied the older man. If he didn't know any better, he would have said that Jake had orchestrated this. But why?

"Why did you send both of us?" Morgan demanded, smelling a rat.

"Always nice to have backup, that way, one of you was bound to do as I asked." Jake accepted both bottles and grinned. "These'll do fine." He looked from one to the other. "No trouble finding them?"

Morgan looked past her father's head. "None."

The look on Wyatt's face was completely innocent. "Nope."

Pleased, Jake nodded. "Good. Now go and enjoy yourselves." Zoe was right. He dearly did love weddings. Almost as much as he loved his kids.

7

Making notes to herself on the yellow pad in front of her, Morgan reached for the mug of coffee on her desk. Then, realizing what she was doing, she pushed it away. No more coffee for her. She was too edgy as it was.

As if anything she found in the bottom of a mug was her problem, she silently mocked herself.

Morgan sighed and closed the folder she'd been working on. God, but she felt exhausted. In the last five days, she'd gotten barely enough sleep to keep a zombie going. Luckily her work wasn't suffering, she thought, rubbing her hand along the back of her neck.

Unfortunately, the same couldn't be said for her sanity.

She supposed it was her own damn fault for letting Wyatt get to her like that. It was turning her emotions and her mind into Swiss cheese. She might rant and rave at him, but here, in the privacy of her own thoughts, she knew there was no excuse for what had happened. She alone was responsible for her own actions and reactions, not some tall, dark, handsome man with a quick grin and an even quicker mouth. A mouth that had reduced her to a palpitating heap of desire.

Morgan silently swore. She should have found enough strength to walk away.

Or crawl away as the case was.

In the deepest part of her soul she'd known, a moment before it'd happened, that once she made love with Wyatt, she'd be plagued by this restlessness, this endless desire to have it happen again. Even though she knew "it" couldn't. Shouldn't.

Wouldn't, she amended fiercely.

Morgan looked down at her hands. She was clutching her pen so hard, her nails were digging into her palm. Disgusted with Wyatt, but mainly with herself, she tossed the pen aside on her desk. It rolled and fell over the side.

Much like her, she thought. Right now, there were people in the case folders on her desk whose lives were far less messed up than hers.

Your own fault, you know that. Your own damn fault, Morgan.

Knowing didn't make it any better. Didn't alleviate the restlessness.

All it seemed to do was intensify the pain she felt radiating through her shoulders. She rotated them, trying to get rid of the ache that was shooting all the way up through the base of her neck into her head. Nothing seemed to be doing any good.

When she felt the hands on her shoulders, kneading the knots out, Morgan sighed like a wayward kitten that had found its way to a life-sustaining shelter in a fierce storm.

"Oh, God, Myra, that feels wonderful." She had thought her assistant, the woman she shared the small office space with, was out to lunch, but obviously she'd made a mistake. Morgan could feel a little of the tension leveling off. "Don't stop."

"I won't," the male voice belonging to her masseur replied with an amused laugh, "but I warn you, I charge by the hour."

Yelping, Morgan swung around. Her elbow caught the edge of her mug, knocking it over and sending lukewarm, chocolate-colored liquid on a quest to soak all of the files spread out on her desk.

"You!" She glared at him accusingly. "What are you doing here?"

Wyatt pulled out two tissues from the dispenser on her desk and quickly applied them to the liquid mess.

"Up until a second ago, I was massaging a pair of very rigid shoulders." He pulled out two more tissues, sending the first two into the trash. "Now I'm mopping up your mess."

Righting her now-empty mug, Morgan quickly pulled file folders out of the way of the oncoming trickle. "Which wouldn't have happened if you hadn't sneaked up on me."

He sent the sopping tissues after the first set. "I

was massaging your shoulders," he pointed out. "How sneaky can that be?"

"In your case, very." Frazzled, Morgan tossed the folders on top of the stack in her in box. "Why—? What—?"

With a hiss of escaping breath, she stopped to collect herself. She hated acting like an imbecile, but after thinking about him almost constantly, to have him materialize behind her was completely unnerving. Taking a deep breath, she let it out slowly before speaking.

"What are you doing here, Wyatt?"

He shrugged, claiming a tiny corner of dried desk for himself by leaning a hip against it. "I was just in the area, and I thought that we might have lunch."

Morgan didn't need to know that he had driven twenty miles out of his way to be here. Because he'd wanted to see her. That was strictly his problem. Caused by her, granted, but still his problem.

It all sounded very suspicious to Morgan. Wyatt had some ulterior motive for being here. He had to. It made her nervous to speculate just what. She hated the way he made her so unsure of herself.

Morgan frowned. "I eat at my desk."

He glanced at the damp marks on the desk that he'd missed.

"That would be my guess." Then he flashed the smile that had originally set her five-year-old heart fluttering. The same smile that had upended her life these past two weeks. "Why not make an exception just once?"

Her eyes narrowed as she remembered what she couldn't force herself to forget. "I already have."

The smile spread further. "I'm talking about lunch, Morgan, not dessert."

Since she couldn't make him leave, she turned her back to him and looked at the computer screen. It could have contained her first lesson in Mandarin Chinese for all the sense it was making to her right now. Wasn't it enough that he had ruined not one, but two of her brothers' weddings for her? Did he have to show up where she worked to haunt her, as well?

For form's sake, she punched several keys before asking, "Why would you want to have lunch with me?"

"To talk," he said seriously.

She scrolled down on the document she wasn't reading. "And if I don't want to?"

He couldn't carry on a conversation with the back of her head. Wyatt turned her chair around so that she faced him.

"Morgan," he said patiently, "not a day in your life has gone by when you didn't want to talk."

A put-down, it figured. She squared her aching shoulders, trying not to wince. "If you came to insult me, you could have saved it for the wedding Saturday."

He grinned. "I've got plenty to spare." Wyatt

looked around the small area. It was made smaller by all the files peering out of the boxes that were lining the walls. He'd never been here before, but it made him think of her. Organized chaos.

There were two framed photographs on the side of her desk, neatly set apart from the mess. There had been a large family portrait taken last year if he remembered correctly. Hank had sent him a copy. Beside it was a small, framed snapshot of a golden-haired boy. Intrigued, Wyatt picked the latter up.

"Put it down," Morgan told him. Not waiting for him to comply, she took the photograph from him. "Didn't your mother ever teach you not to touch things that don't belong to you?"

His eyes slid over her. The word *touch* vividly brought last Saturday to mind—last Saturday, the cellar and a woman with silken skin so exquisitely soft, his very soul had ached.

"No." The single word shimmered between them, more of a promise tied in a memory than an answer. He nodded at the photograph, then picked it up again, putting his body between her and the frame. "Who is he?"

She smiled despite herself. "That's Josh."

He heard the smile and turned to look at her. There was affection in her eyes. Did she know how beautiful she looked like that? "One of your friend's kids?"

If only, she thought. "Josh is nobody's kid."

The words sounded so harsh, it squeezed her heart. "At least, not yet."

She thought of her last visit just this past week. It had seemed so hopeful. And yet a part of her felt sad. Sad because the happier the boy was, the less need there was for her. And she missed him.

"If things go right, though, he's going to be adopted." Her eyes brushed lovingly along the photograph, remembering the day it had been taken. He'd tried so hard to be brave, to be happy. He'd said he knew his mommy and daddy wanted it that way. "He lost both parents in a car crash a little more than six months ago." The shiver came without her realizing it. "I was the first one on the scene. I called the accident in and then went to see if there was anything I could do. But both adults in the car were dead. I found Josh in the back seat, whimpering, holding his mother's hand." Her voice broke, and she flushed. It hurt just to talk about it. She remembered how frightened Josh had been. How much he'd cried. "He wasn't hurt, just very scared. I held him until the paramedics came."

Listening to the emotion in her voice, emotion he had a feeling she had no idea was evident, he saw Morgan in a completely different light. A kernel of admiration put out roots.

"Where is Josh now?"

"In a foster home." She'd worked very hard to screen couples and find him parents who could offer exactly the kind of love Josh needed. It had been far from easy. "They're trying each other on for size." Her eyes narrowed as she looked up at him, realizing what she'd said and how quick he usually was on the uptake. "Leave that line alone," she ordered.

Wyatt smiled amiably, his hands raised in surrender. "Wouldn't touch it." He was more interested in hearing her story than in teasing her. "Why don't you adopt him?"

"Me?" She looked at him in surprise. Had he guessed how she felt about Josh? No, that was far too intuitive for Wyatt.

And yet why else would he suggest that?

"You." He looked at the photograph again before looking down at her. He tried to picture her as a mother and discovered the image was far easier to buy into than he'd thought. The boy even looked a little like her, he mused. "You obviously care about him."

Yes, she did. A great deal. But there were extenuating circumstances. "He's a case." Her voice was crisp, detached. Dismissive.

He wasn't buying it. Why was it so hard for her to admit that she cared? "I don't see any other photographs of other kids. He can't be the only case you have."

She sighed. "I can't adopt him, because in case you haven't noticed, Sherlock, I'm not married. In addition, I'm hardly ever home." She couldn't provide the kind of home life that Josh needed, no matter how much she cared about the boy.

"Out partying?"

She knew he was baiting her. "Working. I work hard at my job, Wyatt." She sniffed, looking down her nose at him. "Unlike some."

He worked hard at what he did. He wouldn't have been the VP of the Computer Programming Division at Tech Corporation if he didn't. But he saw no reason to get into a discussion over it. He would only sound as if he was being defensive. Wyatt picked up the photograph again. "He's a cute boy. How old is he?" He glanced at Morgan. "Four?"

She was surprised that he was right. Most men had trouble guessing correctly. "Right on the money."

His own son would have been four, he thought. Had he survived. Wyatt quietly returned the photograph to its place.

There was something strange about his expression, Morgan noticed, as if Wyatt was somewhere else, thinking. That wasn't like him.

"What?" she prodded, thinking she'd probably regret asking.

Wyatt looked at her innocently, a quizzical look on his face.

She supposed it was her curse to be so curious. "Something about Josh's photograph triggered something in your mind,'' Morgan insisted. ''What?''

No one knew about the child he'd almost had, or his reasons for marrying Judith to begin with. Now wasn't the time to go into it. He shrugged, a glib smile taking over. ''I just never knew there was this softer side to you, that's all.''

Was that a compliment? She doubted it. ''Lot about me you don't know.''

''Apparently.'' Wyatt glanced at his watch. He was going to have to be getting back within an hour if he was to make his three-o'clock meeting. That gave him a little more than an hour to spend with Morgan. ''So, are you up for it?''

Wariness slipped in. She never knew just how to take what Wyatt said. ''Up for what?''

Obviously the woman didn't listen. ''Lunch.''

She glanced at her desk. The work, she knew, would keep. It always did. And she had to admit she was curious about his reasons for seeking her out. She and Wyatt had never socialized—other than at the weddings, she thought ruefully.

''Are you buying?''

He was still old-fashioned that way, but he was surprised that she was. She was right, there was a lot about her he didn't know. And what he had learned had set him on his ear.

Wyatt inclined his head. ''As long as it doesn't offend your sense of independence.''

Morgan took her purse out of the last drawer

and closed it again as she rose to her feet. She slung the purse over her shoulder. "My independence'll survive anything you have to offer."

And the match was on, he thought. He had to admit that in some ways he did enjoy this sparring between them. He held the door open for her.

"Nice to know."

"So what's this all about, Wyatt?" She'd toyed with her diet soda, eaten breadsticks and waited, but Wyatt hadn't said a word about what he was actually doing here. "You've never appeared out of the blue to have lunch with me before."

"True enough," he agreed. Their small talk had lasted all of five minutes, and he had to admit that he'd enjoyed it. She could be pleasant when she wanted to be. "I just wanted to know where we stood."

In her mind that was already settled the only way it could be. "On very firm ground—and far apart from each other."

It bothered him a little that she seemed so detached. "Then last Saturday—"

She raised her eyes from the breadstick she was breaking apart bit by bit and looked at him pointedly. "Was last Saturday. It has nothing to do with the rest of our lives."

On closer scrutiny he realized she wasn't quite as unflappable as she was trying to appear. "Are you so sure?"

"Yes, I'm so sure." Damn him, why did he have to push? Did he want her to bare her soul to him so that he could smugly walk away again? "Wyatt, I don't even like you."

She'd just pushed the envelope too far. "Then why are you here, eating lunch with me?"

Why *was* she here? she upbraided herself. Why did she keep doing things with him she knew she'd regret? Where did this self destructive bent come from? Was it because she felt lonely, watching her brothers leave the single life behind one by one? Or was it that she was just being masochistic?

"Because I was afraid you'd cause a scene at the office if I said no."

He'd sooner believe that Butte was the next capital of the United States. "You, Morgan Cutler, have never been afraid of anything in your life."

Not true, she thought. She was afraid of these feelings she was having. These feelings that all seemed to be centered on him.

"Me, on the other hand," Wyatt continued, "I'm afraid." His eyes met hers, and he felt something tightening inside. "Very afraid."

The words hung in the air between them, beckoning to her, undermining her resolve to remain aloof.

She knew him, he was setting her up, Morgan thought. Setting her up for some kind of a joke, some kind of a fall. Still, believing all that, she couldn't help feeling herself being drawn in.

"Afraid? Of what?"

That was the jackpot question. "Of 'this,' whatever 'this' is." He saw the blank look on her face. "Of what's going on between us," he elaborated. "No matter what you think of me, I don't exactly go on a rampage for conquests to tie to my belt—"

"That describes it rather well," she agreed.

He ignored the quip, he wasn't looking for a fight. He was looking for a truce. "And I certainly wasn't after you."

She popped the last piece of breadstick into her mouth. "I'm flattered."

That hadn't come out the way he'd intended. Nothing had since he'd gotten mixed up with her. Wyatt tried again.

"You're also my best friend's sister. Do you think I think so little of Hank, of all your brothers, that I'd just wantonly pleasure myself with you?"

Now she was angry. "Think so little of Hank, so little of all of them," she echoed incredulously. Where did *she* figure into all of this? "And just what am I, chopped liver?"

He grinned. "No, caviar—with a little crab thrown in. The point is…" Frustration began to scratch at him. "The point is—hell, I don't know what the point is, or why I did what I did—"

She'd never seen him out of his depth before. She could have enjoyed this, if she hadn't been so closely involved in what had happened.

"Just keep piling the flattery on, don't you?"

Morgan pulled her purse to her in the booth. "Lunch is over. I have to get back to work."

He placed his hand over hers. "Lunch just started, I'll drive you back to work, and I haven't finished talking yet."

She was in no mood to be patient. Being near him just reminded her of what she'd done. And what she'd like to do again. That was the worst of it. She wanted to do it again. Because of all the men she'd ever encountered, only Wyatt seemed to linger longer than the moment in her life. Only Wyatt made her ache and dream and want. She didn't like being trapped by her emotions and didn't like being at the mercy of a man she knew she meant nothing to. Even if she had any doubts, he'd all but said as much.

"Yeah, you have. All you're doing is feasting on your foot, and fascinating though that is, I don't have time to sit and watch you do it." His hand moved to her wrist, tightening as she rose. Morgan's eyes grew steely as she looked at him. "Let go of me, Wyatt."

"Then you let go of me."

She stared at him. What was he talking about? "What?"

"You heard me. Let go of me. I can't get you out of my mind. You're there all the time, crowding out everything else." He smiled cryptically. "Sounds just like you, doesn't it?"

It was a lie, all of it, said at her expense. He

was just trying to get her to admit that she had feelings for him. Well, let him do his worst. He'd go to his grave waiting.

Her gaze was cold as she fixed it on him. "I don't know why all the other girls always thought you were so charming. You could definitely do with lessons."

He was tired of games, tired of vying for equal footing. "Maybe I'm not trying to be charming."

"Well, congratulations, you've succeeded brilliantly."

He felt his temper fraying. That hardly ever happened. She really did have a knack for turning him inside out. "Can you drop the act for a minute and just be honest with me?"

Morgan's own temper flashed. It was all she could do to keep her voice down. "What act?"

"The tough little cookie. I've seen your soft center, Morgan. You don't have to pretend with me."

The man was all gall. "I have no idea what you're talking about. Now if you'll excuse me, I—"

But Wyatt wouldn't release her hand. "No, I will *not* excuse you." He saw her staring at him in stunned surprise. "You've messed with my mind and with me, and frankly, Morgan, I don't have a clue what to do about it."

Morgan wasn't buying it, not any of it. Wyatt McCall had too many women in his life competing for his attention. This had to be an act, and although she had no idea what he was up to or why he was doing it, she knew she wasn't about to get ensnared in it.

"It's a fever. Take two aspirins and *don't* call me in the morning." With that, she walked away from the table as quickly as she could.

Morgan was almost at the door before he caught up to her. Taking hold of her arm, Wyatt spun her around to face him. She opened her mouth to ask him what he thought he was doing, but she never got the chance. He kissed her midway between the reception desk and the salad bar. Kissed her in front of everyone who had come to eat lunch at O'Shay's that afternoon. Kissed her long and hard until she was certain that the bottom of her feet had burned a hole in the highly buffed wooden floor.

His heart was racing by the time he pulled away, but he managed to conceal from the one person it would have mattered to. "You accused me of having a fever, I thought I'd share it with you."

This time, Morgan got to watch him walk away. Leaving her completely numb, Wyatt returned to their table without so much as a backward glance in her direction.

Morgan felt the color rise to her cheeks. Muttering a curse about his lineage, Morgan hurried out of the restaurant.

8

He was making her crazy.

Morgan knew that had been Wyatt's intention all along, and she hated admitting, even to herself, that he was succeeding royally, damn him. And the worst part of it was that everyone was beginning to notice that for the past two weeks, she just hadn't been herself.

Who she was heaven only knew. She certainly didn't, not since he'd been messing with her mind. All she knew was that she wanted what she knew wasn't good for her, what she shouldn't want.

He was probably having himself a good laugh over it. Probably? She would have made book on it.

Morgan forced herself to concentrate on the moment, not the man.

The hundred-year-old organ, which had been there longer than the church, was filling the newly refurbished building with the strains of the wedding march. Audra was trying very hard not to trip as she made her way down the aisle in a long gown. Unlike the street-length silver-green dresses that the bridesmaids were wearing, Audra's was white, like her mother's. It had been specifically chosen to signifying that Will was not just making Denise part of his life, but Audra, as well.

Moving slowly, the little girl was scattering soft pink rose pedals along the long, white runner, taking care to distribute them as evenly as she could.

And then it was Morgan's turn. Morgan's turn to walk down the aisle arm in arm with Wyatt. She could feel her stomach tightening as they mutually drew closer to each other.

Three down, one to go after today, she thought as she slipped her arm through his, doing her best to ignore the warmth spreading through her. She already knew that she'd be paired with him again next Saturday. It seemed like the one practical joke her family was perpetually playing on her over and over again each ceremony.

The smile on her lips was forced.

She could get through this, she told herself. After the ceremony and the photographs, she only had to be near Wyatt one more time today. During the first dance. One silly little dance and then she would be free to mingle amid the guests and stay as far away from him as physically possible.

It was a plan. A plan she meant to follow. Why a sense of reluctance washed over her was not something she felt up to exploring.

"You look lovely," Wyatt whispered, just as they drew near the altar.

Startled, Morgan's eyes widened, and she looked at him in surprise.

"What's the punch line?" she murmured softly.

His gaze was long, languid just before they parted. "You tell me," he mouthed.

Now what was that supposed to mean? Why was he giving her riddles on top of a hard time?

Bewildered, Morgan took her place between Fiona and Brianne, trying to make sense of what Wyatt had just said. She couldn't.

She didn't need this, she thought. Didn't need this at all.

Splendid. That was the word to sum up Denise's wedding gown, all right, Morgan thought. Sleeveless, A-line with every inch covered in white appliqué, the gown took Morgan's breath away.

Very slowly, her arm twined with her father's, Denise walked down the aisle toward the man she'd given her heart to. As they joined hands, Denise was beaming.

That was the kind of bride she wanted to be, Morgan thought. A happy one. It didn't matter what she wore or who attended, although she knew she wanted her family there. But as for the rest of it, it could take place in a barn with her wearing burlap as long as the man who slipped the ring on her finger made her heart sing.

There'd never been a man like that in her life,

she thought with regret as the priest began to lead them through the ceremony.

At least, not until…

It felt like a lightning bolt had just zapped right through her. Morgan's eyes darted over toward Wyatt and discovered that he was looking at her.

Oh, God, she was doomed to live alone for the rest of her life.

Pressing her lips together, Morgan looked forward, focusing on Will and Denise. This was their day, not hers. Later, after the reception, she'd think about her solitary destiny, not now.

As the words, the sacred solemnity of the vows, penetrated, Morgan felt a tear slip out. It slid down her cheek before she could stop it.

She was crying, Wyatt realized. He was beginning to see that no matter what she protested to the contrary and how sharp her tongue seemed at times, the woman had a heart like a marshmallow.

It made him smile.

Wyatt thought of the photograph on her desk. The one that had sent him to his phone to call Hank and ask him questions that suddenly needed answers. Of all of them, Hank was the closest to Morgan in age, and Wyatt thought it might give him a vantage point. Besides, Hank was his best friend, and he trusted Hank not to tell Morgan that he was asking about her.

If she found out, it might make things more uncomfortable between them than they already were.

Despite all his promises to himself about never falling into a trap again, he was interested. And maybe just a little bit hooked, as well.

But there was no danger of Morgan springing a trap for him the way Judith had. Morgan would be the one who would set him free if she found him in a trap. He was convinced that she couldn't care less about how he felt. She'd probably laugh if she discovered that he cared.

Just his luck to finally fall for someone, and she hated the sight of him.

Well, not all the time, Wyatt amended silently, thinking of the last two weddings. And she had definitely kissed him back in the restaurant after she'd recovered from her surprise, he recalled.

Maybe the future wasn't as bleak for them as he thought.

"You've been avoiding me."

Anticipation and alarm zipped up and down her spine like two downhill racers. Morgan set down her piece of half-eaten cake on the table. "You noticed."

Since she wasn't turning to him, Wyatt went around to stand in front of her. He knew there were several women at the reception who would have been more than willing to try to make him forget about Morgan, but for this evening, Wyatt didn't want to forget.

"Why?"

Why couldn't the man just let things be and let her continue to avoid him? Why? Because he was Wyatt, that's why. Wyatt, the bane of her existence.

"I'd think that would be obvious. I don't want to get into another compromising situation with you where you could take advantage—"

He took exception to her choice of words. "Who took advantage of who?"

"Whom," she corrected clinging to the sidetrack. "Your grammar's off."

His eyes on hers, he toyed with the large gold hoop that dangled from her ear. Another shiver raced down her spine, heading for home. "That's not the only thing that's off."

She had to get away from him before what was left of her resistance did a nosedive. Spotting Kent, she saw her way out. With determination she made her way toward her brother, Wyatt bringing up the rear.

"This is all very fascinating, but—" her voice drifted to him over her shoulder "—if you'll excuse me, I promised this dance to Kent."

Kent took quick assessment of the situation. "No, you didn't." He beckoned Brianne over. "I've got a very jealous wife." As she joined him, he wrapped his arms around Brianne. "You're on your own, kid," he told Morgan. As an afterthought, he leaned toward her and added, "By the way, did you know he was asking everyone about

you?'' Nodding at Wyatt, Kent danced away with
Brianne, leaving Morgan stranded.

Wyatt caught his lower lip with his teeth. It was
the only thing keeping his jaw from dropping open.
Obviously he couldn't trust the Cutler brothers to
keep a secret. At least, not where their baby sister
was concerned.

She looked at him intently, determined to get at
the truth. ''And just what,'' Morgan wanted to
know, ''have you been asking?''

''Dance with me, we'll look less conspicuous,''
he instructed amiably. Then, not waiting for her to
agree, he took her into his arms, his hips swaying
to the beat. She had no choice but to comply.

It seemed to her that she was doing that a lot
lately, not having any choice, going along with
things.

It had been a late-morning wedding. The reception that followed was being held behind the Cutler
ranch house, with canopies scattered here and there
for those who wanted to get out of the sun. Will
and Quint had put up a temporary dance floor, and
it was there that Wyatt was leading her.

Because she didn't want to draw any unneces-
sary attention, she waited until they were dancing.
A whole new set of problems arose, but since they
all had to do with her, she tried desperately to ignore them.

''Why are you pumping my brothers about
me?'' she demanded.

He laughed. "A couple of questions can hardly be called pumping."

She'd be the judge of that. Why was he asking anything at all? They'd known each other most of their lives. He knew everything about her that needed knowing. "What kind of questions?"

He pretended to think. He could see the color rising to her cheeks again.

If he'd lived to be a hundred, Wyatt would have never thought he would see Morgan blushing. Just showed that you learned something every day. He spun her around the floor and then pulled her back into his arms. "You like me, don't you, Morgan." He made it a statement.

Of all the egotistical, big-headed... If she'd been entertaining thoughts along that line, he'd made them evaporate. "I what?"

"You like me," he repeated. He saw Morgan's eyes darken to a deeper shade of blue. Storm warnings, he mused. "Don't worry, it's not all one-sided. I like you, too."

As if that mattered to her. Morgan ignored the slight leap her heart made and frowned. "Very big of you."

"I think so." Wyatt looked into her eyes, and the teasing smile faded into something serious. "I mean it, you know. I'm not sure if it was at Hank's wedding or Kent's, but you've suddenly become a very real, very vibrant woman for me. And I like what I find." He paused as Morgan struggled with an unexpected bout of speechlessness. "Or maybe it was at the hospital."

The reference jolted her back to reality. "The hospital?"

Wyatt nodded, guiding Morgan around another couple. "You remember, that day your father had his heart attack."

Morgan knew she'd never forget one second of that awful day even if she lived forever. She stiffened, trying to avoid the feel of Wyatt's hand on her back. She remembered how afraid she'd been and how vulnerable. And what he'd said to shatter her world and make her feel like a fool. How dare he try to make that into something special now?

"What I remember is that I poured out my heart to you, you kissed me and then told me you were getting married—*that's* what I remember."

He'd told her the truth back then because for a glimmer of a moment, he'd felt something for her. Felt that just possibly, there might have even been something between them, given the chance, but it had already been too late.

"One thing didn't have anything to do with the other. You were telling me about how afraid you were that your father was going to die. My getting married didn't affect that one way or another."

But it did. It had torn out her heart just at the moment she'd wanted to offer it to him. He'd been kind to her, kind and concerned, and the antagonism between them had transformed into something else. Something equally as charged but far more compelling. Until he'd told her about Judith.

Morgan drew back and studied him. "You don't have a clue, do you?"

Lost. He felt he was lost again. It happened a lot around her. The woman should come with a road map and a manual of instructions. "Where you're concerned? Guilty as charged."

Morgan didn't want to trade quips, not when her heart was so heavily involved. Instead, rather than say anything in response, she slipped her hands from his and walked away from him.

Wyatt stared at her back. He wasn't conscious of any of the people who were looking in his direction. All he was conscious of was that Morgan was walking away from him. Again.

He caught up to her in three strides and took hold of her arm, marshaling her over to the side away from most prying stares. He saw indignation flash in her eyes, but he wasn't about to give her a chance to use that lethal mouth of hers. Not for a dressing down, at any rate.

"Seems to me that in the last three weeks, I've seen enough of your back, Morgan, to last me a lifetime," he declared in hushed tones against her ear.

Morgan pulled her head away. "I don't know what you're talking about."

The hell she didn't. "You keep walking away from me."

And she was going to keep right on walking. "Emphasis on the word *away*."

This time Wyatt wasn't going to give up and let her go. This time he wanted to undo the tangle of misunderstanding that existed between them. "I didn't force myself on you."

Morgan refused to let Wyatt say that she had wanted him. That it was true didn't matter, she wasn't going to feed his ego; it was just what he wanted. "You caught me off guard, remember?"

The excuse only stretched so far. "The first second." Wyatt held up his index finger. "What's your excuse after that?" He realized that he'd raised his voice, so he lowered it. "Well?"

Morgan pressed her lips together ruefully. "I'm working on it."

She could work on it from now until doomsday, it didn't change the facts. "The truth is, Cutler, you don't have an excuse. You wanted to make love with me."

And now he was gloating about it. What had she expected? She glanced around to see if anyone had overheard them. But no one seemed to be listening. At least that was going in her favor.

"So, I have self-destructive tendencies." Her chin jutted out defiantly, daring Wyatt to make something of this. "So what?"

"Why is it self-destructive?"

What else could it be? He certainly didn't want a long-term relationship. "Well, whatever's between us isn't going to go anywhere, is it?'' she demanded. Then her voice softened just a tad. "Is it?" she repeated.

Smooth lines didn't seem appropriate here. And oddly he was out of them, at any rate.

"I don't know." The hurt look in her eyes cut him to the quick. He caught her wrist just as she started to leave again. He wasn't finished. "What I do know is that when you're not around, you're still around for me."

More double-talk. Morgan sighed. "I'm not in the mood for riddles."

Why did she keep twisting things around? "It's not a riddle, it's a fact. You keep lingering on my mind, Morgan." Suddenly he had to make her understand. And maybe if he could make her understand, he could make himself understand it, as well. "Like smoke long after the fire's died down."

The analogy hit her the wrong way. "So now I'm a burned-out forest fire?"

He laughed shortly. Served him right for getting involved with her in the first place. But now that he was, he couldn't seem to shake himself loose.

"I don't know what you are, Morgan," he told her honestly. "Except for on my mind night and day."

He didn't want her walking away again. He didn't want anything else in this world, except to be with her. Oh, God, he had to be losing his mind, he thought. He wasn't making any sense. None of this made any sense to him.

His eyes held hers before he said, "Make love with me, Morgan."

She had to be hearing things. Yet he looked deadly serious. Morgan looked around. The reception area was filled with family and friends. Most of the town was here, for heaven's sake. His parents were a few yards away, talking to their other son, Casey. Wyatt had to be laughing at her.

"Where? Right here, where everyone can see?" Morgan tried desperately to hide the mounting quaver in her voice.

"No," he said softly. He looked behind her toward the back door. "In your room."

"My room?" Did he have a death wish? If anyone came in on them, she'd never live it down. "I—"

Wyatt laid a finger to her lips, stilling her protest, an entreaty in his eyes.

Morgan sighed, surrendering long before she uttered a word.

Her breath brushed along his skin, heightening his excitement, his anticipation.

"I must be crazy," she murmured.

Wyatt smiled at her. "Then that would make two of us."

Somehow, there was a comfort in that. Without a word Morgan took his hand and led him to the back door. Opening it, she slipped inside.

Wyatt followed. He had no choice. She still had his hand.

Jake slid the healthy slab of wedding cake onto his plate, but his attention was elsewhere. Nudging his wife, he pointed toward the back door, sparing not a little pride.

"Looks like I started something."

He looked as if his chest was going to bust out of the tuxedo. Zoe smiled indulgently, patting his arm. Why did men always think that they were the movers and the shakers?

"You didn't start anything, old man." To soften the words, Zoe brushed a kiss against his cheek.

He took a different view of the events. "Oh, then who did?"

She didn't hesitate. "Nature." Zoe did a little quick calculation in her head. "Springing a trap that was twenty years in the making I suspect."

"You can't tell me I didn't help oil that trap a little. What do you say, after we send the newly-weds on their way, you and I take a little stroll down memory lane and relive our own wedding night?"

"You mean relive fumbling in the dark for the first time?"

"I never fumbled," he protested, his mouth curving generously.

Her smile matched his as she rested her head on

his shoulder. She loved this man with all her heart and hoped that her children would be as lucky in their choice of mate as she was with hers.

"No," she agreed, "you never did."

9

Sixteen, that was the age Wyatt made her feel. Morgan felt as if she were sixteen again, sneaking into her room for a necking session while her parents were out of the house, instead of a full-grown woman with a serious career and responsibilities.

There was more to it than that, Morgan thought, making her way up the stairs. Wyatt didn't just make her feel as if she were sixteen, he made her feel, period. Feel things she'd given up hope of ever feeling. The very prospect was exhilarating and frightening at the same time.

She'd waited all her life for this to happen, to have a feeling sustain itself for more than what seemed like a few minutes. There'd never been a shortage of men in her life. But they had all failed to keep the attraction going. She'd always lost interest so quickly she'd begun to secretly believe there was something wrong with her. She'd never met any man who measured up to the shadows her brothers cast, never met anyone who had made her yearn to see them again. Yearn to be in a moment that contained them in it, as well.

Coming to the landing, she glanced at Wyatt. Glanced at him and felt the excitement bubble anew within her veins. Even though she'd tried to avoid him because of the complications that were involved, secretly, deep down where she lived, she *wanted* to see Wyatt. Wanted to be near him.

There was no point in lying to herself. She wanted to make love with him again.

Why, of all the men in the world, did it have to be this one who lit her flame? She knew she meant nothing to Wyatt beyond a challenge. Why then couldn't she just walk away?

Because she couldn't. It was as simple as that.

But the parade of weddings would be over next week, and then her life would return to normal. Whatever "normal" was.

The prospect didn't cheer her.

Morgan softly closed the door to her room. The sound of the lock slipping into place echoed in her head.

Prelude to a Seduction, she thought. But who was seducing whom?

Wyatt looked around the small bedroom. He'd peered into the room countless times throughout the years, usually sticking his head in to get off a teasing remark at his friend's pesky kid sister.

All that seemed like a hundred years ago, happening in another lifetime to someone else. Certainly not to him.

She was nervous, he realized. It would have been hard for him to envision that, if he hadn't been here to see it. But there was an uneasy look in her eyes, as if she had suddenly thought better of what she was doing. Heaven, he hoped not.

Wyatt slipped his arms around her and drew Morgan closer to him. A delicious tension began to hum through him. "Change your mind?"

A dozen times since she'd taken his hand. All the way up the stairs she'd been involved in an internal debate that had bordered on an argument.

Morgan cocked her head, looking at him, searching for answers to questions she hadn't fully formed. "And if I did?"

Ever so lightly, Wyatt pressed a kiss to the side of her throat. Her pulse jumped, telling him that she was just as much a prisoner of these feelings as he was. It helped some, knowing that. Knowing that he wasn't the only one in this heavenly hell he found himself.

He sighed. "I'd be forced to take a cold shower while you went out to rejoin the party."

Morgan studied his face, trying to discern if he was just saying what he thought she wanted to hear. "And that's it?"

"That's it—" mischief glinted in his eyes "—unless you wanted to hang around to dry me off." He whispered another kiss to her throat, this time on the opposite side. "In which case I think we might skip the shower altogether. Or take it together."

It was hard forming words, hard thinking, when desire burned such holes in her, but she needed to have at least some things cleared up. He was coming off terribly noble. There had to be a flaw.

"You wouldn't call me a tease and then—"

He stopped kissing her and looked at Morgan. Was she asking what he thought she was asking?

"And then what? Force myself on you?" The smile faded. She couldn't be serious. That wasn't his way. It never had been. "Hey, Morgan, even when you claimed not to like me, you knew me better than that."

Yes, she thought, she knew him better than that. The one thing she did know about Wyatt McCall was that he wasn't the kind of man who'd force himself on a woman. But then, he didn't have to. As far as she knew, no one'd ever refused him. And she no longer could lay claim to that honor.

It bothered her a great deal that she was just part of a group.

What had she expected? To be placed on a pedestal? She'd known where she stood with Wyatt before any of this had begun. Sexy, silver-tongued, charming, the man never indulged in games.

And then Morgan's eyes narrowed. "What do you mean, I 'claimed' not to like you? Are you saying that I liked you?"

He knew that tone. She was spoiling for a fight. Maybe to alleviate her guilt over having feelings for him, he didn't know and he was in no mood to analyze it, not when his hands begged to touch her, not when his lips ached to kiss her and his body yearned for the feel of hers.

"Morgan," he said softly, his fingers lightly gliding along her face, seducing her senses, "I don't want to argue with you. I don't want to trade words or go five rounds. Let's just say that you win, okay?"

"Win?" She pounced on the word. "So now you're a prize?"

That wasn't what he meant. Wyatt grinned. "If you say so. But what I was talking about is that I was surrendering and that you won whatever confrontation you thought we were having." He feathered a light network of kisses along her face, reducing her to a barely standing, quickly dissolving liquid mass of hot needs. "I really don't want to fight."

Her heart was beating so hard, she could hardly hear herself. "Make love, not war?"

He smiled, and the smile seeped into her senses. "That's the general idea."

Morgan wanted to give in, wanted to surrender, but she had to know. "Why me?"

Once again he stopped, but this time only for a moment before he resumed brushing his lips along the column of her neck.

"Hunting for a compliment? Okay, I'll give you one. Because of all the women I've ever met, you're the only one who's ever lingered on my mind, the only one who keeps haunting me."

Morgan forced herself to rally. She wasn't going to go the way of all the others before her. She wanted to be different. She *would* be different.

"Doesn't say much for Judith, does it?" She dared him to lie to her.

This time it was Wyatt who drew back. Hearing his ex-wife's name was like having cold water dashed in his face. Maybe this was a bad time, after all.

"Judith is a closed chapter in my life. Let it be, Morgan."

But because he wanted her to, she couldn't. Couldn't shy away from what she knew was reality.

"Why? Because I'd find out that you said the same things to her?"

He'd never said the same things to Judith because he'd never felt the same things about Judith. He never lied about his feelings. To lie somehow seemed reprehensibly dishonorable, and honor meant a great deal to him.

She'd probably laugh if he told her that, he thought. So he didn't protest, instead he answered with a question of his own. "Would it bother you if I did?"

Morgan tried to appear indifferent. "No." Indifference melted before the truth. "Yes." But that was giving too much of herself away. Morgan sighed, helpless. "I don't know."

That, too, made two of them. Although in his case he felt as if he were coming closer to the truth.

"Always liked multiple choice. Gives me an even chance at getting the right answer." And then the teasing smile faded. He framed her face in his hands, looking into her eyes. They were still as beautiful as they'd been when he first noticed them, five years ago, on a cloudy day as they'd stood in the hospital parking lot. "If it matters, I never felt about Judith the way I seem to be feeling about you."

He'd qualified it with a single word. *Seem.* But even that wasn't enough.

"Then why did you marry her?" When he didn't answer, Morgan had the answer she'd thought she would get. "I thought so."

She left him completely confused. "Thought what?"

Morgan crossed to the window. It faced the front of the house. There were no wedding guests here, nothing to remind her that she should be downstairs, not here. Nothing but her own sense of honor.

"That you're lying to me." Suddenly she hated Judith. Hated any woman who had been as close to Wyatt as she herself had been. And hated him for letting her get that close. What was happening to her? Was she losing her mind? "That you probably told her the earth moved and the stars shone brighter and—"

Angry, he told her the reason before he could stop himself. "I married Judith because she was pregnant, and she said the baby was mine. And it probably was." He'd had no reason to doubt her.

For a second Morgan was completely speechless. "But you don't—"

"—have any kids?" He second-guessed her question. "No, I don't." Maybe it meant something that he was telling her, Wyatt thought. In any event, he'd blurted out half of it. She might as well know the rest. "She miscarried in her sixth month. It was a boy." He'd had a son, a son he'd never gotten to hold, a son he'd loved from the moment he'd found out about his existence.

Confusion assaulted her. It didn't make any sense. Her brothers would have said something to her. This was too big a secret to have kept to themselves.

"But she never showed—"

Wyatt was well aware of that. It had been the basis of the first arguments he'd had with Judith.

"That would be because of her vanity. Judith practically starved herself, trying to hang on to that figure of hers for as long as she could." Her flagrant disregard of nutrition was what had directly contributed to her miscarriage.

It didn't make any sense to Morgan. In this day

and age, there were options. "Why didn't she just—"

He knew what she was going to ask. It was something he refused to even consider.

"Religion's a powerful thing at times. It makes itself known in our lives when we least expect it. She couldn't bring herself to be the one to make the decision to end a life." Judith had turned to him for that, but he'd surprised her by refusing to sanction the termination of his child. There was no way he would have had her sweep the tiny life away. Instead, he'd proposed.

His mouth hardened. "But she could very well starve it away."

It was the truth. He was telling her the truth. What's more, he still grieved for the lost life. Why no one else knew no longer mattered. Morgan's heart ached for him.

She placed her hand on his shoulder. "Wyatt, I'm so sorry."

He looked at her and saw the sympathy. It slammed into him with both fists, and he turned away, shrugging. Sympathy disarmed him.

"Yeah, me, too."

She paused, but she knew she'd have no peace until she found out. "That still doesn't answer my question, though."

He'd lost track. Wyatt shoved his hands into his pockets. "Which one?"

"Why did you marry her?" Morgan circled

around him so that she could see his eyes when he answered. "A lot of people have kids these days and they don't get married."

Just because it happened to others didn't make it his way. "I'm not a lot of people, Morgan. I had this quaint notion that my kid deserved to start out with a complete set of parents." It was all a moot point now. "That maybe I could give him the kind of home you had."

The longing she heard in his voice surprised her. "Me?"

Wyatt shrugged. "You, Hank, Quint, the others." Did that really surprise her? "Why do you think Casey and I hung around here so much?"

She'd never thought about it much. It was just a given. "I thought you liked my brothers—and tormenting me."

He laughed, coming up behind her and slipping his arms around her waist. He liked holding her this way, he thought. There was something comforting about it.

"That goes without saying, but I also loved the feeling here. The love, the warmth." He thought back. "Hell, you can feel it the second you walk through the door." In all the years, that hadn't changed. He still preferred being here to his own parents' house. "Even when there was yelling, it was the kind of yelling that made you feel loved, not the kind that made you feel like you were a fool. Or worse, an intruder."

Morgan turned around to face him. She'd never pictured him as experiencing one insecure moment in his life. "Is that how you felt?"

He didn't want to go on talking, not when she felt this good in his arms. "Hey, haven't you run out of questions yet? When's my turn?"

Morgan twined her arms around his neck, feeling touched. He'd let her have a peek into his soul, a soul she hadn't even realized until just now that he had. And she felt closer to him. She knew she might live to regret it, but there were already so many regrets involved here, what was one more?

"I think it's coming up right now." Rising on her toes, she pressed her mouth to his.

The urgency happened a second after contact and remained throughout, egging them on until they were enveloped in a frenzy. Clothes were discarded, needs faced and met, and hungers, hungers were almost sated. Almost, but not quite. A little remained to remind them that there was always more to be had.

Later.

For now, they lay on her bed, spent, contented and confused.

He slipped his arm around her, drawing her against him. Even now he felt himself responding to her. Another first. To make love and want to do it again almost immediately. What sort of hold did she have on him?

Morgan turned her body into his. "We're going to have to stop meeting like this."

He laughed at the melodramatic line and kissed the top of her head. "Why?"

That was affection, she thought. Not desire, not passion, just pure affection. Her heart felt as if it was glowing. "Because someone's bound to walk in on us."

"Oh, I dunno. I've always been a pretty lucky guy." He lightly swept his hand along the swell of her hips, stirring her. Stirring himself. "I figure my luck'll stretch a little further."

She was trying very hard not to succumb to the desire he'd aroused in her. They had to be getting back. "Oh, I forgot who I was dealing with. Casanova."

"At the risk of shattering my image, I haven't been with as many women as you think I have." He laughed at the thought. "Actually, I don't think it's physically possible for any one man to have had as many encounters as you attribute to me."

She would really love to believe that, believe that there hadn't been a legion of women in his life, Morgan thought as they both rose and dressed. "You're not exactly a novice."

He'd be lying if he pretended that. "No, *that* I'm not." His eyes met hers. "Does that bother you?"

She sniffed. "Couldn't care less."

He lifted her chin, keeping her from looking away. "Is that so?"

"Yes, that's so." Morgan was finding it difficult to keep a straight face. If she kept giving herself away like this, how could she make him believe that he hadn't tangled her heart up?

"Seems to me I tasted something quite apart from indifference in your kiss." To prove it, he brushed a kiss against her lips.

Morgan moaned despite herself. Rising on her toes again, she wrapped her arms around his neck and pressed her lips against his in earnest.

"Morgan, are you in there?"

A light rap against the door preceded it being opened. Quint's jaw dropped as he looked into the room.

Morgan froze for exactly half a heartbeat. Yelping, she jumped back, her heart thudding against her rib cage.

Rubbing the back of his neck, Quint looked off into space. He didn't know if he was more stunned or pleased by the turn of events. Hell of an awkward moment. "Sorry, didn't know you were...busy."

Morgan could hear the grin working its way forward in her brother's voice. "You breathe a word of this to anyone—"

Quint didn't have to look at her to know the expression on her face was dark.

"No danger of that." Shaking his head, he

laughed. "I don't think anyone would believe me. I saw you, and *I* still don't believe me." Morgan and Wyatt. Wait until he told the others. "How long has this been going on?"

She resented the implication. "It's not 'going on,'" Morgan corrected tersely. "I just had something in my eye, that's all."

"And he was doing what?" Quint asked.

Thinking about it, Quint figured this was probably a long time in coming. He was sorry he'd walked in on it and spoiled things for the two of them. Who knew where they might have gone if he hadn't come looking for Morgan.

"Quint—"

"What?"

"Shut up," she ordered tersely.

"Good idea." He began to turn toward the door. "In any event, I'd better get out of the line of fire before the fireworks start."

"No, I'm getting out," Morgan announced as she hurried out of the room. "Not a word," she flung over her shoulder, "or Ginny's going to be a widow before she's a bride."

"Threatening the sheriff's against the law," Quint called after her.

A deep chuckle underlined his words. But as Wyatt passed him on his way out the door, Quint clamped a hand on the younger man's shoulder. Wyatt stopped, a quizzical look on his face.

"I've always liked you, Wyatt, but you hurt her

and I'll have to shoot you. Don't make me waste any ammunition. I hate having to fill out forms."

"Quint—"

"I don't know what's going on between you and her, other than the obvious, but I don't want any casualties when it's over, understood?"

Wyatt had a feeling he'd get the same speech from all of her brothers. He liked to think he would have felt the same way himself if he'd had a sister. In any case, Quint had nothing to worry about. "I've no intentions of hurting her, Quint."

Quint figured it was a significant choice of words. "What are your intentions?"

Damned if he knew. "I'm still working that out." He saw that Quint believed him. "All of this is as big a surprise to me as it is to you."

Quint damn well could have been knocked over by the breeze made by a butterfly's wings when he'd walked into the room. "Oh, I don't think so, Wyatt." He paused, reflecting. "Do you love her?"

Did he love her? Yes, he supposed that might be the word to attach to this feeling. He was so new at it, he wasn't sure. But that was a moot point. "It doesn't matter how I feel. Morgan won't have anything to do with me."

"Didn't look that way to me."

But Wyatt hadn't been talking about the obvious. "Other than a physical attraction—"

Quint never cared to see an animal suffer. And

not a full-grown man, either. He threw his friend a lifeline. ''We talking about the same woman? My little sister might seem to be all temper and emotion, but she's got a pretty good handle on things. If it's happening between the two of you, it's because she wants it to happen. My guess is that you both want it to. And my advice is that you don't waste any more time than you already have. Clear the air once and for all, tell her what you feel.'' He looked at him intently, his expression softening. ''Tell *yourself* how you feel,'' he added. ''You'll be glad you did.''

Wyatt sincerely had his doubts about that. Once he confronted his feelings, really confronted them, there'd be no place to hide. He didn't look forward to having his gut kicked in any more than it already had been.

10

━━◄━

"It's nice of you to pitch in like this, Morgan."

Zoe took out the wedding decorations that had been taken down last Sunday morning. She'd ignored Jake's "helpful" solution of leaving the decorations up the entire four weeks. He saw no reason to keep duplicating work.

Men and their shortcuts, she thought fondly.

Zoe handed the first box over to Morgan. Her daughter had surprised her by showing up early this morning, saying she'd taken the day off from work and wanted to help.

Zoe took out another carton, this one filled with streamers.

"I could certainly use the extra hands. Three of your brothers are off, setting up housekeeping for themselves, and Lord only knows what's happened to Quint." When she'd heard the front door open this morning, she had expected to see Quint walk in, not Morgan.

"He's probably busy. He *is* the sheriff, Ma," Morgan pointed out.

Zoe carefully extracted a white tablecloth from the depths of the closet. Her voice echoed back to Morgan. "In a town where the most notorious crime is shoplifting cupcakes."

Which, Morgan knew, was the way that Quint had met Ginny. She'd come sailing into Serendipity after Quint had locked up her kid sister, Jennifer. Not so much for shoplifting cupcakes from the grocery store as for her hell-bent-on-rebellion attitude—which, he'd told Morgan, reminded him a great deal of her, when she was that age. The difference being that she had a whole family to fall back on.

Now Jennifer and Ginny were both living here, and Ginny was Serendipity's first lawyer.

That would make Quint and Ginny law and order, Morgan mused with a smile. Hefting the box of decorations, she carried them to the back porch.

And what were she and Wyatt? she wondered, walking back inside.

Chaos and disaster, probably.

"Where are you?"

Morgan blinked and looked up to see that her mother had stopped working and was looking at her quizzically. "Right here, Ma, helping you."

Zoe had a different take on that. Piling the three tablecloths one on top of the other, she handed them to Morgan.

"Your body might be taking up space here, but you definitely aren't here in mind or spirit." She peered at Morgan's face. Her daughter's eyes were troubled. "Anything you want to talk about?"

Morgan neatly turned on her heel and walked out to place the tablecloths beside the box. Her voice floated back to Zoe.

"No."

Zoe waited until Morgan returned. "Anything you don't want to talk about but I should hear, anyway?"

Morgan smiled, remembering. That had always been her mother's standard line when she was growing up. The one she used to extract the truth about some prank or other out of her. It had been a long time in between pranks since then.

"No, Ma, there's nothing. Really."

Zoe knew better. Following Morgan outside with the last of the decorations, Zoe said. "Wyatt McCall can hardly be called nothing."

The box Morgan was carrying nearly slipped from her fingers.

"Who told you?" And how much had they told her? If Quint had inadvertently said anything to their mother about walking in on them, sheriff or not, she was going to kill him.

Triumph curved Zoe's mouth, a mouth that she'd passed on to her daughter. "Nobody. I just guessed." Very carefully she began laying out the various decorations on the first table. She glanced at Morgan. "Correctly, by your vehement reaction.'' She smoothed out a crepe streamer. ''I always thought the two of you belonged together.''

Morgan sighed. She looked up at the sky. Cloudless and blue, it promised them a beautiful day for the wedding tomorrow. ''Then you'd be the only one. He's not interested in settling down.''

So, her daughter was thinking along those lines, was she? All her birds were leaving the nest at once. It took her breath away.

Zoe abandoned the crepe streamers and slipped her arm around Morgan's shoulders, giving her a comforting squeeze.

''How do you know? Just because he's had one bad marriage doesn't mean he's soured on the whole institution.'' That wouldn't be like Wyatt, and Zoe prided herself on being a good judge of character. ''I've watched that boy over the years, Morgan. He's always hung around, looking hungry for what we had here. His folks are very nice and polite, but they're not very demonstrative people.''

For the life of her, Zoe could never understand people who didn't feel the need to hug their children, to express with a touch what they were feeling. She looked into her daughter's eyes.

''I think he likes fire, Morgan, and Lord knows you've got plenty of it to spare. Warm him up a little.'' When she smiled a certain way, she looked young enough to be Morgan's sister. ''Not that I think he needs any lessons in that department.''

Now there was an understatement. "I'll keep it in mind."

"Good." Zoe got back to work. "I'll hang on to the decorations."

She'd always said her mother was an optimist. And never more than now. As much as she wanted to hold on to a thread of a fantasy, Morgan knew better.

"Better keep them in an airtight box so they'll keep a long time," Morgan advised as she went to get the ladder.

Zoe watched her go. "Won't be that long," she murmured under her breath.

"If your face were any longer, you'd run a risk of getting splinters from the porch floor."

Startled at the sound of his voice, Morgan looked up. She'd been so engrossed in thought, sitting out here on the front porch, she hadn't heard Wyatt approach, hadn't seen him park his car in the driveway. The phone call she'd just taken not ten minutes ago was weighing heavily on her. The way she felt right now, she would have missed hearing a twenty-piece marching band work its way up the walk.

Damn, why did these kind of things happen to helpless children?

Pressing her lips together, she frowned in Wyatt's direction. "Did you come up all this way just to insult me?"

"No, I didn't even know you were going to be here." He tapped the thick box under his arm. "I came by to drop off Hank's—Hank and Fiona's wedding proofs," he amended. God, but it was hard thinking of his best friend as being one half of a couple. He studied her expression. She looked upset. "What's wrong?"

Morgan waved a hand at the question. "You don't want to hear." And she didn't feel like going into it right now. She was afraid she'd cry if she did. Cry because she knew Josh was going to be hurt again after she'd promised him that he never would be again. He was going to think she lied to him.

Wyatt came onto the porch and leaned against the railing. He wasn't going anywhere until she talked. "I asked, didn't I?"

She swallowed the retort that came to her. He was acting civil, the least she could do was behave the same way.

"Josh's foster parents can't adopt him, after all." Even as she said the words, she could envision Josh's small face when she broke the news to him. "They can't even keep him through the weekend. He's going to have to go back to the Home."

The Home. The term had all the warmth of metal left out on a January night. It was a place where he would have a bed and food for his belly, but nothing for the void that existed in his life.

"What happened?"

Was it her imagination, or had his voice softened as he asked? "Ann's mother's taken ill. She and Ray want to refocus their attention on preserving the quality of her mother's life." Morgan knew the kinds of financial burdens that were involved. There was no way there would be money left over to take care of a small boy who wouldn't stay small for long. "They're going to New Mexico to bring her back with them to live. That leaves Josh completely out of the picture."

Wyatt thought of the photograph on her desk. And how he would feel if it were his son who'd been orphaned. "Isn't there someone else who could adopt him?"

She'd already exhausted the possibilities before finding the Jacksons. "People want babies, not half-grown boys."

Four hardly seemed that, yet he knew she was right. It was her job to be right.

Wyatt nodded, absorbing the information. Thinking. "Why don't you bring him to the wedding?"

The suggestion startled her. That was what she'd decided on just now. She was hoping the outing tomorrow would help soften the blow a little for Josh.

She cocked her head, looking at Wyatt. "You taken up mind reading?"

He laughed. "Don't flatter me, Morgan. I'd need more than eight years of college and a Ph.D. before

I could attempt to divine what's on that mind of yours." He straightened, his hand tightening around the rectangular box. "Your folks inside?"

She turned around to face the door. "C'mon, I'll take you to them. I want to see those pictures, too. What are you doing with them, anyway?"

"Running an errand. Your mother asked me to pick them up if I got a chance." Reaching the door ahead of her, he held it open for Morgan. "You coming?"

"Said I was, didn't I?"

"You've been known to change your mind."

It felt as if he'd whispered the words against her hair just as she passed him. Morgan tried not to shiver. Why did he do that to her, make warmth skim along her like that?

"Not that fast."

"Yes, that fast," he contradicted. "You keep changing it all the time around me."

She looked at him significantly. "That's because I keep coming back to my senses and then leaving them again."

He'd have expected nothing less ambiguous from her. "Which is which?"

Morgan thought it safer not to elaborate on that.

Morgan hurried into the hot pink gown as quickly as possible. The last of the four bridesmaids dresses, she mused, angling to pull up the zipper.

Always a bridesmaid, never a bride.

The old saying echoed in her head again, the way it had the first time.

She didn't have time for old sayings, she thought, fumbling with her headpiece. She had a small boy waiting for her. She didn't want to leave Josh outside for too long, even though the boy was with her father. She knew Josh felt better when she was around.

He'd taken the news incredibly well that his adoption had fallen through. There were times she thought he was far older than his tender years. Adversity did that. If she had her way, he would never know another moment of pain or sorrow.

But she couldn't have her way, she reminded herself. For now, all she could do was make this as pleasant a day as possible for Josh. She'd taken her with him to the one formal-wear store they had in Serendipity and managed to rent a small tuxedo for him.

It had been a little large, but a few nips and tucks here and there had made the fit acceptable. She wanted him to feel a part of things. She might not be able to legally adopt him, but she could damn well go through all the motions of giving him a family life.

Stepping into her shoes, Morgan pulled open the door of the tiny room off the altar and walked into the hallway. Her father was right where he was supposed to be and was talking to Father Gannon, but Josh was no longer at his side. He was nowhere to be seen.

Wonderful, he'd wandered off.

Morgan glanced at her wristwatch. The wedding was about to start in less than fifteen minutes. She had to find him. Fast.

She tapped her father's arm. "Dad, where's Josh?"

The concern in her voice pleased Jake. There were times he worried that of all his children, Morgan was the one who felt the least.

"Wyatt took him."

"Wyatt?" Why would Wyatt take Josh anywhere?

Jake nodded. "Said he wanted to get acquainted. Try the parking lot," he suggested when she just stood there, confused.

Good a place as any to start looking, she supposed. Gathering up the folds of the tight skirt, Morgan quickly made her way outside. She wasn't aware of the pleased smile on her father's face as he watched her.

Rounding the church, she found Josh at the rear of the building. With Wyatt, just as her father'd said. They were playing catch.

For a second, Morgan watched them, the boy and the man, astounded and admittedly touched. They looked so natural together. Was this what Wyatt would have been like with his own son had the boy lived?

She felt a pang for him.

Now there was a surprise, her feeling sorry for Wyatt. It had to be a day for miracles.

"You'll get dirty," she called out to them as she came closer. She glanced at her watch again. Time was racing by.

Wyatt's hand curved around the ball. He motioned to Josh.

"C'mon, we'd better get inside. The show's probably going to start soon." The boy hurried to his side and Wyatt draped an arm around his thin shoulders. But his attention was on Morgan. "I can remember a ragtag girl who didn't care if she was covered with dirt from head to foot," he reminded her.

If he were to guess now, he would have said that she'd probably begun to win his heart then. Every inch a determined tomboy, she'd been like no other female he'd ever come across.

"Well, that ragtag girl didn't have to walk down the aisle at her brother's wedding," Morgan pointed out. She paused to brush a speck of dust off his collar. "And neither did you."

Wyatt waited until she was finished. "So, am I presentable?"

She pretended to brushed another speck off his shoulder. "You'll do."

His eyes met hers. "Will I, Morgan?"

He was asking her something she wasn't prepared to answer. Or maybe she just thought he was. "They're waiting on us."

"Wyatt said he's going to adopt me," Josh told her as she took his hand.

That brought her to a skidding stop. What was this all about?

"What?" As Josh repeated his statement, Morgan could only stare incredulously at Wyatt. "When was this decided?" she demanded.

She looked annoyed. So much for being able to pick up signals. But Wyatt remained firm.

"Probably when I looked at his photograph on your desk. I make snap judgments, then let them cool off before I act on them. When you said his foster parents were forced to back out, I figured it was a sign."

"Of what?" she wanted to know. "Your insanity?" How dare he toy with Josh's emotions. "You're not even married."

"Don't have to be these days," he told her simply. "Not if you can show that you can properly support a child. Besides, Josh and I have bonded." He grinned down at the little boy. "Right, Josh?"

Bonded? They'd hardly been together for ten minutes. "Over one ball game?"

"We talked." He had all the proof he needed that this was right. The light in Josh's eyes. Maybe this was what he'd needed all along, to be responsible for someone else. "The ball was extraneous."

So was his brain, she thought. Morgan set her mouth hard. The last thing she wanted was for Wyatt to fill Josh's head with false hopes. He'd been disappointed too many times as it was.

"*We'll* talk," she promised Wyatt tersely.

Holding Josh's hand, she hurried into the church ahead of Wyatt.

He watched her walk away from him, the way he'd done so many times these past four weeks.

"I'm counting on it," he said to her back.

It was hard keeping her mind on the wedding, even though it was even more splendid than the ones that had come before. It was as if her parents felt that since this was the last one, the impression it made would have to last a long while.

Ginny's sister, Jennifer, was her maid of honor, and Quint had included their cousin, Carly, who was also his deputy, to balance out the bridal party. Once more Audra was the flower girl, strewing rose petals along the white runner with joyful abandon.

Morgan waited for their cue. But just before she and Wyatt were to begin walking down the aisle, Wyatt put his hand out to hold her back. Confused, she looked at him. Before she could ask what was going on, she saw Josh being ushered forward by Denise's father.

Josh looked nervous, but he was beaming.

Pillow in hand, with two rings dead center on it, Josh looked to Wyatt, not her, for guidance.

"Just like we practiced," Wyatt whispered, flashing a smile at the boy.

Practiced? When had this happened? Just what had gone on while she'd been in that tiny room, changing?

Morgan leaned into Wyatt. "Who decided to make him ring bearer?" she whispered.

"I did." He'd used an old pillow Father Gannon found in the rectory. It had been left over from a previous wedding. "I thought it was a nice touch. Couldn't let his miniature tux go to waste, could we?" He felt her looking at him. They should have begun walking. "What?"

Something warm slipped over her. A warm, fuzzy feeling she would have never associated with Wyatt. "You can be nice when you want to be, can't you?"

"Been telling you that all along," he murmured just as Josh reached his destination. It was their turn to walk. "Show time."

Morgan caught herself looking forward to the first dance. Looking forward to an excuse to be close to Wyatt. Yes, it certainly was a day for miracles, she thought.

When he took her in his arms, she felt as if she'd come home. Morgan had to concentrate not to let herself slip into the feeling that beckoned to her.

"I want to thank you."

He looked at her, mildly surprised. "For anything in particular?"

"Yes." She wasn't going to let him tease her out of this. "For being nice to Josh." She hesitated for a moment before continuing. For once, she didn't want to sound as if she was criticizing him. "But you really shouldn't toy with his emotions like that."

She'd lost him, but then, that was nothing new. "When did I do that?"

"When you told him that you'd adopt him."

"I was serious."

Despite what she'd seen earlier, she found it hard to believe. He was a ladies' man, a charmer. Where did a child figure into his plans?

"But, Wyatt, you're a single man," she reminded him again.

He laughed at the way she said it. "It's not like it was a terminal condition."

Something froze inside her. "Then you have someone in mind?" *Surprise. Just like the last time,* a voice echoed in her head.

Except that this time she'd really gone and done it, she'd made love with him, and now he was going to tell her that he was marrying someone else.

Hurt, wanting to be anywhere but here, Morgan stopped dancing and began to pull away.

But Wyatt held her fast. "Dance isn't over yet."

She didn't care about any stupid dance. How

could he do this to her, play her like she was some little fool?

Maybe because she was.

Morgan struggled to keep the angry tears from flowing. "Let go of me, or I swear I'll hurt you."

"If that's the way you accept proposals, no wonder no one's ever asked you."

It took a minute for the words to catch up with her brain. And even then she didn't think she'd heard him correctly.

"What proposal?" she demanded. "What are you talking about?"

"If you'd let me get in a few words edgewise, maybe you'd know." He took a deep breath. This was harder than he'd thought. Because this time his heart was in it, and he was afraid of having it rejected. "I'm trying to ask you to marry me."

It was a joke. It had to be a joke. She wanted it too much, so it couldn't be happening. "Why would you be doing that?"

"So that when I bring you to the church for the wedding, you won't be caught completely off guard," he deadpanned.

This was Quint's wedding. She couldn't start a riot in the middle of it, she reminded herself. And she didn't want to scare Josh. But she really did want to punch Wyatt, just once, for laughing at her this way.

"What kind of a sick joke is this?"

"I didn't know they came in varieties." As she

pulled, he tightened his grip. Enough was enough. "Morgan, will you marry me?"

The anger, the hurt, slipped away. Shock and disbelief took their place. "You're serious."

He held his right hand up, silently swearing an oath. "Never more."

"You're asking me to marry you," she reiterated. "Just like that?"

Amusement began to blanket his initial unease. "Would you like me to take out a billboard?"

"No, I'd like you to make some sense."

"What, asking you to marry me doesn't make sense? It makes perfect sense. We already know how to fight—" a sexy glint entered his eyes "—certainly know how to make love, and we're both crazy about your family." He glanced over toward where Josh was playing with Audra. "And Josh. What more is there?"

He *was* serious, she thought. But he had forgotten something. Something very important. "There's a little matter of love."

"It's not such a little matter," he contradicted. "It's a large matter." And because it was, she deserved the unvarnished truth. Even if it made him uncomfortable. "Morgan, I think I've probably loved you for a very long time."

An eighth of a feather could have knocked her over. "Then why didn't you ever say anything?"

There was a simple reason for that. "Because in the beginning, I didn't realize that I was. And because you'd have laughed at me. Or knocked my head off.''

She opened her mouth to protest, then shut it. He had a point.

"You're probably right about the second part. But why now? Why do you suddenly realize you love me now?" She had to know, had to hear it. And then maybe, just maybe, she would believe it.

He'd thought about it, long and hard. "Because I saw the way you looked when you talked about Josh. And how much it bothered you not to be able to take him in, not to give him your love. I realized you'd make a good mother. That you weren't just sexy as hell, you were loving, as well." He looked into her eyes. Looked and saw his destiny. "I want a big family, Morgan. The kind of family you grew up in. And I want you to be the mother."

"Is that how you see me, as the mother?"

His grin was wicked, reminding her of the stolen moments they'd shared in the wine cellar and in her room. "I think you already know the answer to that one."

She considered his proposal for the space of time it took to draw a breath. "I guess I could do worse than marry you."

It seemed to him that he was the one doing all the giving here. "You're going to have to do better than that for an answer, or the proposal's null and void."

"I guess marrying you is all right?" she offered, a smile playing on her lips.

"Better." She knew what he wanted to hear, Wyatt thought. "Try again."

Amusement rose to her eyes. "I love you?"

"It sounds better if you don't make it sound like a question."

"You are a demanding soul, aren't you?"

"At times," he allowed.

"All right." Pausing, she looked into his eyes. "I love you." The words came out in a soft whisper. "Maybe I always did."

"Much better."

She rose on her toes to kiss him, still swaying to the beat. "You might just have something there, for a change, McCall."

His arms tightened around her. His smile enveloped her. "I think so."

"Think someone should tell them the music's stopped?" Jake asked Zoe.

Zoe turned to look at her daughter and the man she'd always secretly known would be her son-in-law. "No, let them enjoy themselves." She smiled. "Looks like we've got one more wedding in the offing, old man."

Pleased as punch, Jake grinned. "Looks like."

Epilogue

———◆———

"How come none of you told me?" Morgan looked from one sister-in-law to the next. There were four of them now, four Mrs. Cutlers surrounding her in the tiny room, all newlyweds, all resplendent in light turquoise gowns shot through with silver threads that caught the light and gleamed warmly.

"Told you what?" Fiona, the most nurturing of them, fussed with Morgan's veil, straightening it. Despite her high heels, she had to stand on her toes to reach the crown.

Morgan pressed a hand to her stomach, careful not to get the engagement ring Wyatt had given her caught on the appliqué. It flashed at her, reminding her of the look in his eyes as he'd slipped it on her finger. "That I would feel less nervous walking down Main Street naked than I feel right at this minute."

Brianne grinned impishly. "We wanted to save that as a surprise. Smile." Unable to help herself, she'd brought a small camera with her into the vestibule and aimed it now at Morgan.

Before Morgan had a chance to raise her hand, the flash went off.

"Oh, great, now I won't be able to see the mess as I throw up." She felt her empty stomach knotting in protest against all the butterflies that were meandering back and forth within it like 747s circling in an unending holding pattern over a fogged-in airport.

Denise laced her arm around Morgan's shoulders and gave her a quick, heartfelt squeeze. "You're going to be fine, Morgan. You're not going to throw up, and your eyesight's going to be back to normal before you take those first steps down the aisle."

The first steps toward the rest of her life...the rest of her life. Morgan took a deep breath, but panic still flared. "Oh, God, what if I'm making a mistake?"

"You really believe that?" Ginny fixed Morgan with her sternest look, the one she used in court when she was intent on getting the truth out of a hostile witness.

It worked. Morgan slowly shook her head. "No. No, I don't."

A strange calmness began to take hold of Morgan. This wasn't a mistake. She'd made a lot of them in her life, but this was not one of them. It might very well be the single best thing she'd ever done, outside of adopting Josh.

There was a light rap on the door, and it opened a crack.

"Tight fit," Denise laughed, she maneuvered open the door and squeezed out. As she passed him, she brushed a kiss on her new father-in-law's cheek. "Hi, Dad."

"Make sure she doesn't bolt, Dad," Brianne warned playfully, mimicking Denise and brushing a kiss on his cheek.

"See you up front." Ginny followed her sisters-in-law and kissed Jake.

"'Bye, Dad," Fiona murmured before she kissed him, too, and disappeared.

"Well, just you and me, girl." Jake looked at his daughter, feeling as if he was going to burst with pride. She looked beautiful. Just like her mother had on their wedding day. "You ready?"

Morgan pressed her lips together. "As I'll ever be."

The strains of the wedding march were beginning. "I believe they're playing your song." Jake presented his arm to her.

She slipped her arm through it, her heart starting to pound in anticipation.

"I've only got one request." Jake's lips barely moved as he began to walk down the aisle with her.

"And that is?" Morgan whispered back.

"That you name the first baby after me."

A smile played on her lips. "What if it's a girl?"

"Hey, I'm open-minded. Couldn't have survived with all of you if I weren't."

She tried not to laugh. It wouldn't look right. "I'll talk to Wyatt."

Jake suppressed a chuckle himself. "You'd better do more than talk if I'm going to get that grandbaby."

"I always listen to my daddy."

Her eyes fixed on Wyatt, she saw him turn in her direction when she was a little less than halfway there. Turn and smile as he looked at her. The pounding in her chest sped up, but she didn't feel like bolting anymore. Didn't feel like being anywhere but where she was. Walking to her destiny.

Stopping at the altar, Jake placed Morgan's hand on Wyatt's arm and stepped back.

"What kept you?" Wyatt whispered to her with a smile.

She felt his smile spread over her heart. "I'm not sure anymore."

But the main thing, she thought, was that she was finally here at his side. Where she belonged.

*   *   *   *   *

Books by Marie Ferrarella

Books by Marie Ferrarella writing as Marie Nicole

If you enjoyed what you just read,
then we've got an offer you can't resist!

Take 2 bestselling love stories FREE!

Plus get a FREE surprise gift!

Silhouette Romance
proudly presents
an all-new, original series...

Six friends
dream of
marrying their
bosses in this delightful
new series

Come see how each month, office romances lead to
happily-ever-after for six friends.

In January 1999—
THE BOSS AND THE BEAUTY by Donna Clayton

In February 1999—
THE NIGHT BEFORE BABY by Karen Rose Smith

In March 1999—
HUSBAND FROM 9 to 5 by Susan Meier

In April 1999—
THE EXECUTIVE'S BABY by Robin Wells

In May 1999—
THE MARRIAGE MERGER by Vivian Leiber

In June 1999—
I MARRIED THE BOSS by Laura Anthony

Only from

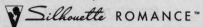

Silhouette ROMANCE™

Available wherever Silhouette books are sold.

Look for a new and exciting series from Harlequin!

HARLEQUIN
Duets™

Two __new__ full-length novels in one book, from some of your favorite authors!

Starting in May, each month we'll be bringing you two new books, each book containing two brand-new stories about the lighter side of love! Double the pleasure, double the romance, for less than the cost of two regular romance titles!

Look for these two new Harlequin Duets™ titles in May 1999:

Book 1:
WITH A STETSON AND A SMILE
by Vicki Lewis Thompson
THE BRIDESMAID'S BET
by Christie Ridgway

Book 2:
KIDNAPPED? by Jacqueline Diamond
I GOT YOU, BABE by Bonnie Tucker

**2 GREAT
STORIES BY
2 GREAT
AUTHORS
FOR 1 LOW
PRICE!**

Don't miss it! Available May 1999 at your favorite retail outlet.

HARLEQUIN®
Makes any time special.™

Look us up on-line at: http://www.romance.net   HDGENR

Silhouette

SPECIAL EDITION™

In March 1999 watch for a brand-new
book in the beloved MacGregor series:

THE PERFECT NEIGHBOR
(SSE#1232)

by

#1 *New York Times* **bestselling author**

NORA ROBERTS

Brooding loner Preston McQuinn wants nothing more
to do with love, until his vivacious neighbor, Cybil
Campbell, barges into his secluded life—and his heart.

**Also, watch for the MacGregor stories
where it all began in the exciting 2-in-1 edition!**

Coming in April 1999:

THE MacGREGORS: Daniel—Ian

Available at your favorite retail outlet,
only from

Silhouette®

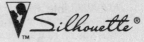

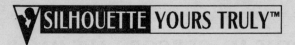

Sneak Previews of April titles
from Yours Truly™:

BORROWED BABY
by Leslie Davis Guccione

Columnist Nick Hansen had the perfect idea for a story:
Who was more appealing, single men or single fathers?
The only way to find out was to do an experiment—
with himself as the guinea pig. So he borrowed his
nephew and did a little research. Then he met beautiful
Shannon McEvoy, and knew the single dads had won.
He hadn't meant to deceive her—or fall in love with her.
And when she found out he was lying, she refused to even
speak to him. Now he had to find a way to make it up to
her before he lost the only woman he'd ever want as the
mother of his *real* children.

FIANCÉ FOR THE NIGHT
by Melissa McClone

When Cassandra Daniels asked Troy McKnight to be her
temporary fiancé, she had no idea of the havoc it would
wreak on both their lives. She had done it only to prove
to her parents that she could find a decent, upstanding
man to share her life with. But she never expected her
folks to actually *like* him—and even start planning their
wedding! They were worlds apart, with nothing in
common except the bar in which they'd met. So why
was she all of a sudden falling for a man she had
planned on knowing only for a night?